Also by Jack Bennett

JAMIE

Mister Fisherman

Mister Fisherman

JACK BENNETT

LITTLE, BROWN AND COMPANY · BOSTON · TORONTO

FOR MY PARENTS

Mister Fisherman

PROLOGUE

For two years during the Depression he was a ghillie, an angler's boy, down at Plettenberg Bay. It was a good part of the country with wide white beaches and high dark rocks and a wide bay with blue mountains on the eastern shore.

In those days there was a big blue-pointer shark always feeding around the point at Robberg, a big tongue of land and scrub-covered rock which stuck a mile straight into the sea like a breakwater. On Robberg itself there were small buck and hares living in the low heather and tight twisted willows. There were all sorts of game fish off the point, and a great many sharks. Out on the point you were very remote from the land. You were right out in the blue deep water. When the westerlies blew the big ocean swells came fifty feet up the rocks, the whole sea bulging up and spilling over the rocks and falling back roaring white.

This big blue-pointer that stayed around the point they called the Blue Train and it was a legend up and down the coast. Nobody ever caught it.

Pillay was out on the point one day with a young man up from Cape Town. He had very good and expensive American tackle and he said he was going to catch the Blue Train. He said this in the bar of the Beacon Island Hotel one night and everyone laughed. He was the sort of beginner angler who

7

thought that luck and good tackle were all you needed. He was also a man who took himself very seriously and when they laughed at him he became very annoyed and went to bed early in a huff. He lay awake for a long time listening to the waves break on the rocks below his window. When the sea was quiet he could hear the men in the bar below. It quite spoiled his night.

The next day Pillay took him out to the point. It was a hot day and they started late because the young man did not like getting up early. He complained about the length of the walk and about the sand, which was hot and burnt him through his canvas shoes.

When they reached the point the young man sat down in the shade and Pillay fixed the tackle.

'I'm after shark,' said the young man. 'I'm going to get that big shark they say hangs around here. You'd better make up the tackle for it.'

Pillay looked at him and thought Heaven help us but here's where a lot of tackle goes into the sea. He made up the tackle with a twelve-o flat-sided Zane Grey hook on a four foot wire trace and threaded a mackerel on to it, tying the tail up near the eye of the hook with twine so that it wouldn't slide down. The young man sat and watched him.

'What's it look like?' he asked. The sea was a clouded blue. There had been a west wind the night before and some rain up in the mountains and the rivers had come down.

'Okay,' said Pillay. 'Shark water. Too dirty for yellow-tail.'

'That's what I want,' said the young man.

He nodded and smiled with satisfaction. 'That's what I want.'

Pillay put the bait out and wedged the rod butt into the rocks and as he turned away the reel screamed and the tip went over in a tight bow and stayed there. The young man woke up and gave the fish the stick very hard and then the line went slack. He reeled in and the mackerel was gone.

'He was big,' said Pillay. 'You hit him too soon.'

'He was big,' said the young man. 'I felt him when I sticked him. He was a big boy, all right.'

Pillay put on a fresh mackerel and put the bait out again and in ten seconds the reel was screaming and the young man was laying into the fish with the big stick all right and his eyes were popping with excitement and then the trace parted and the line fell slack in the water. The young man reeled in without saying anything and handed the rod silently to Pillay.

On the third cast the Blue Train took the bait just after it hit the water. The hook pulled out after one jump. By now the young man was very annoyed indeed and Pillay thought he was going to throw the rod into the sea. It was rather funny and Pillay wanted badly to laugh. But he kept his face very solemn and baited up again.

'He's very *skelm*, that fish,' he said.

'I'll say,' said the young man, with feeling. He was thinking of the bar that night.

The Blue Train was still waiting and he took the fourth bait right on top with a swirl and a splash. The young man's eyes got very wide when he saw the size of the shark but he

9

put the old stick in and the Blue Train put his head down and ran for the deep blue and the reel sung high wide and loud and the young man tightened up the screw-drag – there were no star-drags in those days – and clamped the leather hand-brake against the drum but the Blue Train never faltered. He peeled the eighteen-cord off the drum until the green backing-line was showing and then he whipped through the backing-line and the eighteen-cord hummed like a zither and then broke showww! and Pillay sat on the rocks and laughed until his stomach hurt.

The young man didn't say anything. He put the rod down very carefully and wiped his face with his handkerchief. Pillay packed the tackle and they walked slowly back. The sun was right overhead and it was hotter than ever.

They didn't speak until they were over the roughest part of the berg and down on the beach path.

'That's never happened to me before,' said the young man.

'Cleaned out like that, I mean. Everything! I couldn't hold him. You know that? I just couldn't hold him.'

He could not get over the fact that he had been unable to hold the fish. He kept shaking his head and saying that he couldn't hold it.

They came down on to the hard-packed beach and walked along towards the hotel. The tide was out and there was a wide wet gleam along the beach. Near the hotel three boats lay canted over on their bilge keels. Out in the bay they could see the line-boats bobbing in the swells around Blind Rocks.

'That's never happened to me before,' said the young man.

'You want to go out tomorrow, Boss?' asked Pillay.

'Not for that boy. Certainly not for that boy.'

'We can go for kob,' said Pillay.

'Okay. For kob, then. But not for that boy. Did you see how he broke me? Man, I just couldn't stop him.'

'That Blue Train's a big boy,' said Pillay.

'I'll say,' said the young man with feeling. He was thinking that he would not go down to the bar that night.

After the Depression came the war and Pillay joined the Merchant Navy from a fishing port up in Angola and after a year he was accepted into the navy and posted to mine-sweepers.

The little ships worked the coast from Lobito Bay high up on the western shank of Southern Africa to Lourenço Marques on the palm-green eastern side. During those years they swept a lot of mines and took a great many seas green off the Wild Coast. After the war he came back to South Africa and worked in the harbours, bossing the dock gangs in Cape Town and in Durban for a while.

He worked on the railways, too, as a bedding boy, although he was old for the job, and did a spell on the Blue Train and on the Orange Express. He liked trains almost as much as he liked boats. He was on a train into Port Elizabeth one time and he had to wait a day for another train out to Johannesburg. That evening he walked down to the harbour and saw an old sweeper berthed near the naval base.

She was rusty and leaned tiredly against the jetty but he recognised her. He walked around to the naval base and crept under the barbed-wire and when he was close to her he saw the old number painted-out on her bows. He was standing there looking at her when the watchman came up and asked him what the hell he was doing on defence force property and if he wanted trouble. He said he didn't want trouble but that this old can was his boat, his own boat that he'd last seen in Lourenço Marques Bay when they took him ashore with malaria and after that they'd posted him to a new sweeper which was never as friendly.

The watchman spat in the water and walked back to his cabin. Pillay went aboard and walked alone all over the dark and empty ship until he thought his heart would burst and then he walked slowly back along the jetty. It was now quite dark and the lights were on and shining in the water. Across the harbour a Union-Castle liner was being pulled away from the quayside. She was lit from stem to stern and her funnel was bright orange in the floodlights. As he watched the tugs backed away and the liner sounded her whistle: BAAAROO-MMMMM . . .BAAROOMMM explosively across the silent harbour. He watched her turn seawards and walked slowly off the jetty. The watchman was waiting for him. He stuck his head out of his cabin. He was a thin sour man in his late forties.

'You kiss her good-bye?' he said. His voice was a sneer. Pillay walked on the gravel at the end of the jetty and lifted the barbed-wire.

'She'll be gone tomorrow,' shouted the watchman. He had followed Pillay to the edge of the jetty. 'Tomorrow they're takin' her out and sinkin' her.'

Pillay slipped under the wire and walked back to the station. He lay in the baggage car without talking to anyone until the train pulled out. He was not angry or hurt or sulking. He was just remembering.

12

Soon after that he'd packed up working on the trains and gone back to the harbours. Just before his fiftieth birthday he had enough money to buy a small boat. He hitched lifts up the Tzitzikama coast and found what he wanted and a place to work it from and he never went back to the harbours or the trains.

1

On this summer morning he was up and out before sunrise and walking on the dew-damp sand beneath the willow-trees before the birds were awake. The stars were still out and the spiky willow-branches were black against the dark blue sky. When he came out of the trees and stood on the open flats he could see the first pale wash of yellow along the horizon and the riding-lights of a trawler anchored on the dark side of the bay under the hills. He walked towards the sea. The heather was waist-high and scraped dryly against his boots and trousers.

He stopped on the edge of the cliff, where the sand-path twisted down through a low frieze of wind-warped willows, and smelled the sea, turning his head and flaring his nostrils until he could smell the sea-smell right at the back of his nose and in his throat. It was still dark, but far out he could see the liquid flicker of sea-phosphorus.

He stood listening to the heavy sigh of the Indian Ocean swell around the rocks two hundred feet below. His feet had crushed the scrubby heather and the fallen willow leaves and he could smell these smells too, but they were part of the whole sea-smell.

He put down his dented billycan and laid the heavy coil of stiff blooded line beside it and lit a cigarette. Then he picked up the billycan again and walked carefully down the steep dark path, placing his feet from memory. The path looped along the face of the cliff, passing above the white-painted cottages of the tourist fishing camp.

In one of the cottages a light was on and he saw someone moving behind the curtain, the shadow distorted against the cloth.

When he reached the small harbour the sky was turning blue overhead and the seabirds were crying. There was a soft breeze coming across the sea and the oil-slicked water was snuffling gently at the low breakwater.

The boy was waiting for him. He sucked hard on his cigarette and filled his lungs with smoke and threw the stub into the water. The boy was sitting on a bollard with the tip of his short expensive game rod poking over his shoulder.

'You're late,' he said.

'I'm sorry,' said Pillay. He put down his billycan and blood-line and loosened the rope on the bollard and started to haul the boat's bow alongside. The boy stood watching him.

'Do you think we'll get the katonkel?' he asked while the serang made the boat fast. The old man lifted his big shoulders.

'Some. Maybe. They was in the bay. Perhaps they still here.'

'We'd better,' said the boy, who was going to university that year and feeling very much a man, 'we'd bloody better.'

Pillay loaded the rods and the boy climbed down into the boat. It was getting light now and he read the name painted on the bow.

'That's a hell of a name for a boat,' he said. '*Poor Man's Friend*. What sort of a name is that?'

Pillay was filling the tank with red power paraffin from a

battered oil can. He put the lid back on the tank and stowed the empty can under the thwart.

'Just a name,' he said. He primed the carburettor and swung the starting handle and the engine fired on the third swing and he opened the pull-throttle slightly to warm it. When she was running evenly he checked that the cooling pump was working and then dropped the bow and stern ropes and put her astern, edging slowly away from the jetty, and swung the bow seawards. The noise of the exhaust bubbled away across the harbour and echoed from the sea-wall.

He put the engine ahead and they slid slowly across the oily water. Once they were beyond the lee of the wall the boat began to move slightly in the small sea and a few drops of spray spattered inboard.

The sun was just above the horizon and the wind was cold with the sharp fresh chill of early mornings on the sea. The serang sat at the tiller and watched the boy clipping the expensive American reel on to the expensive game rod and thought, this will be a long day.

He watched the boy and thought, how can I explain the name of this boat to this boy, this rich boy from Johannesburg? To him all boats are toys to be bought by his father.

He had named the boat *Poor Man's Friend* because that was what it was, to him. He was a poor man, and the boat was his friend. When he spoke of the boat he always called it by its name; he never prefixed it with 'the', or said it in inverted commas, the way people usually do when they talk about boats.

Poor Man's Friend was a clinker-built double-ender by Thesen's of Knysna, a good strong sea-boat with a stubby mast and loose-foot sail, built with all the old Norwegian skill, and the serang loved her.

Through the hard years on the docks and in the holds of many ships he had dreamed of owning his own boat and coming away from the city to this high wild coast with the purple heather and dark pines on the steep hills and the long swell running up the black rocks.

Now they were well clear of the harbour and he turned south, running out towards the deep blue water of the warm current which runs down the African coast from Mozambique. The sun was higher and the breeze had died, leaving the sea very flat.

Very high overhead there were some streaky clouds, very white and thin. Today will be a good day, he said to himself, looking along the crinkled blue line of the horizon, sharp in the bright air. There may be a wind from the west later, but I don't think it will be a big one, and before it comes it will be a good day. He had fished along the coast for many years and he was seldom wrong about the weather.

He looked back towards the yellow beach and the creamy frill of the surf and the red iron roofs of the little town. Pale blue smoke was drifting from several chimneys, and the sun glanced back at him from curtained windows.

Outside the tourist cottages he could see people pulling a small boat on a trailer along the dusty road. He wondered in which cottage the boy's parents were living.

Behind the cottages the land reared up steeply into sandstone cliffs. Behind the cliffs were the fretted tops of the pine plantations. Further inland the Tzitzikama range rose up like a wall.

18

There was cloud around some of the blue peaks. Lower down was the misty purple of early heather, showing up against the dark green forests. The new fire-belt ran across the mountain slopes like a fresh scar. It had just been chopped and burned off. Soon it would start healing. The new green growth would cover the black burn and the fire-belt would just be a pale strip through the trees.

There was a dirt road up over the hills into the valley beyond. The road looped up through the forests and skirted the shoulder of the tallest mountain you could see from the bay. It went through a natural gap in the range, a poort.

On one of the nearer hills the name of a village had been spelled out in huge letters, using whitewashed boulders. The villagers were very proud of the sign, probably because it had been hard work making, and the stones were always kept whitewashed. You could not read the name from the bay, but the white blur showed up among the heather.

From the national road below the village you could read the name. It did not attract many people to the village, though. The village was a double row of grey stone cottages with dark-thatched roofs and a wide red earth street between.

The people of the village were Coloured. The men worked in the Government plantations or ran boats out from the rocky coast near Bloubaai.

Sometimes they came into the town to buy lines or hooks or clothes. They were silent men with dark lined faces and they never spoke to anyone in the town except the shopkeepers.

They just bought what they wanted and went away again,

walking up through the heather to the village below the white stone sign.

'Which cottage are your people in?' he asked the boy. The boy was tying a fancy-looking feathered lure on to his plaited line. He looked up, impatience tugging at his mouth.

'Oh, one of them. You can't see it from here.' He finished fiddling with the lure and laid the rod down across the thwart so that the lure dangled just above the water.

'Can't we go any faster?'

'Full speed now,' said the serang. The boy looked at the clattering two-cylinder engine and shook his head.

'Plenty of time,' said the serang. 'Still early yet.'

He hooked the tiller under one arm and took off his jersey and then his old blue seaman's shirt, enjoying the feel of the sun on his body.

He was sixty that year and his body was still hard, wide and deep in the chest with heavy shoulders. Only around the belly was there any fat, and that was thick, healthy fat, not the watery fat of old age. He looked down at his body and thought that being poor might not make a man comfortable, but it kept him from becoming soft.

He laid his hands down in his lap, palms upwards, and flexed the fingers. I have been very lucky, he thought. My body is still strong, and my hands are real good fisherman's hands. They were broad and thick fingered, of the texture of wood which has been soaked in sea-water and then allowed to dry quickly in a hot sun: deep-cracked and hard, with the colour bleached out of the palms by work and water.

They were a long way out now, and they could see the mountains behind the cliffs, long folded ranges, deep blue in the distance, with the deep green patches of pines showing on the nearer foothills.

Beneath them the water was blue-black with depth. Looking over the gunwale the old man could see shafts of sunlight driving into the depths.

He put his hand in and felt that the water was warm. There was a lot of plankton in the water. He could see it catching the rays of sunlight, like dust motes in a darkened room. That was a good sign.

He picked up his blood-line and looped a tattered red-feathered lure, scarred by the teeth of many fish, on to the short wire trace.

'We can go,' he said to the boy. 'Good water here.' He dropped the lure over the stern and let the line run out slowly through the fingers of his left hand. He could feel the oscillation of the lure in the water. The boy came aft and rested his rod on the transom and clicked off the drag on the big reel and let his lure run out astern. When he had it about fifty yards out he cut in the drag and tightened it.

'Don't do that,' said the serang. 'Not too tight. Big fish take you sudden, and whoooom!'

The boy smiled at him.

'Suppose you just worry about your handline?' he said. He patted the reel. 'There's nothing's going to bust me on this little outfit.'

His blue eyes were impatiently angry. Who does this coolie think he's teaching how to fish? he thought.

He looked at the coiled bloodline and smiled thinly. A handline fisherman. He had heard that the coast fishermen, the professional boatmen, were good fishermen and good seamen, but he had been out in a good many boats with his father and had never met one who'd impressed him.

'You caught katonkel before?' asked Pillay. The boy looked up and laughed shortly.

'No. Only tunny. And a sailfish.'

'I don't know 'bout tunny,' said Pillay. 'But these katonkel, they're fast. They take you so quick you don't know what hit you. You got that drag too tight, they bust you before you can get it off.'

'A tunny's fast,' said the boy. 'A tunny's damn fast. I don't reckon a katonkel's going to do any more than a tunny.'

He ran the red feather tail of the lure through his fingers, smoothing it.

'These katonkel. They're what they call barracuda up in Natal?'

'Yes. But he's not really a barracuda. Proper barracuda's a different fish. Don't get them so far south.'

'These katonkel. How big do they come?'

'Oh, forty, maybe fifty pounds. But not often. Usually they run about twenty-five, thirty. But they can go. They don't need much weight. They can go like hell.'

'That's not very big,' said the boy. 'Hell, that's not so very big. I've caught tunny bigger than that. I don't think a katonkel can be better.'

He sat dangling the red-feathered lure that fishermen call a feather jig. It turned slowly and shone in the sunlight where the serang had scraped the oxidation away with his knife to expose the raw shining lead underneath.

Pillay looked at the jig. They always know everything, he thought. This sort always know everything. He lifted his eyes slowly and looked at the boy's thin tanned face with the lips set straight and saw all the confidence in the world stamped on the face so clearly you felt you could peel it off like a mask. They're always like that, the rich. Nothing ever goes wrong for them and they never expect it to. Everything falls right first time.

'Well, you just take it easy with the first one,' he said. 'I'm not making a joke. These katonkel are fast, fast, man, faster than anything you've ever seen. You don't lose him on the first run, then you'll be okay. He's got no side play. He's just fast.'

'Katonkel, smatonkel,' said the boy. 'You bloody boatmen are all the same. Any game fish scares the pants off you.'

His eyes were full of contempt.

'I'm just warning you,' said Pillay. 'You can't say afterwards that I didn't warn you. It's your gear.'

'Like I said,' said the boy, 'why don't you just worry about your own line?'

He settled himself on the thwart and hooked the butt of the rod under his thigh.

'Need a fighting chair,' he said. He was not used to fishing in boats without all the amenities.

'How the hell can you catch game fish from a boat with no chair?'

'They cost money,' said Pillay.

He was trying very hard not to get annoyed. He wanted to enjoy this day. The weather looked good, he was being well paid and he didn't want to spoil everything by getting annoyed.

So he shrugged and watched the boy sitting astride the

thwart with the butt of the rod between his thighs. He felt the hot feeling of irritation in his stomach and tried to ignore it because to show it would be bad for business and the twenty rand which the boy's father was paying for this day, and others to come, he hoped, was good business.

It was now mid-morning and a bad time for fishing and they had had no strikes. There was a grey haze and the sea was calm as an oil-slicked harbour. The serang dozed in the sun and sensed the boy's growing impatience at the slowness of the fishing.

The boy's face was burned an angry red by the sun and there were flakes of loose skin on his cheeks. His name was Faraday Koenig and his father had nearly as much money as anyone in Johannesburg, which was a lot of money indeed, a fact which had made Faraday popular at school and which he sensed, although he scarcely admitted it to himself, would make him popular at university. He was looking forward to going to university. He had all the confidence of the rich compounded with a quick mind and a good unfumbling pair of hands on the rugby field and a personality completely without sensitivity, attributes which make for a happy life at school or university, at least in the world in which Faraday moved.

He was slouching across the thwart, sensuously lapped by the sun and his anticipations, when the fish hit his lure and pulled the rod down sharply against the gunwale, with a hard imperative rap which woke him with a start.

He snapped out the clutch and braked the spinning drum with his hand while he tightened the big star drag and swung around so that he faced aft. The serang was sitting up and watching him, pulling in his handline without taking his eyes from the boy.

'Now,' he said. 'Now. Hit him.'

The boy dropped the rod tip on to the gunwale and heaved back hard and there was a high twang from the line and the white game rod curved and then suddenly straightened as the hook came away and the line fell slack in the water. Faraday reeled in the line without speaking and the serang picked up the lure and looked at the thin shining scars on the metal.

'Katonkel?' asked the boy. He was very angry at missing the fish.

'Maybe,' said the serang. 'Looked like it. Could be hammer-head. Lot of them around now.' He dropped the lure over the stern and the boy let it stream astern.

The boy lost two more strikes in quick succession, eager-ness making him strike too soon, and then he connected with a small katonkel which came alongside without much fight, making only two short runs.

The serang scooped it neatly out of the water with the short gaff and it lay shimmering green and blue and silver on the floorboards, smacking the deck with short shivers of its swallow tail.

The serang hit it above the eyes with his kierie and the colours glazed and muddied and the beauty went out of it.

Then the serang caught two in quick succession, twenty pounders, letting them run and then snubbing the heavy bloodline around his hand and stopping them short.

Faraday missed another and landed a small bonito and at noon the fish stopped striking and the lures glinted and fluttered untouched in the clear water.

They had been running south at about four knots and now the serang opened the throttle slightly and turned north-west to bring them back towards the coast, lost in the low grey haze. He turned his head to get a bearing from the sun and saw the white flashes of diving birds to the south. He looked shorewards again, hoping that the boy had not seen them, but Faraday was shading his eyes with his hand, squinting through the glare from the sea.

'Birds,' he said, pointing. 'Diving. Doesn't that mean fish?'

'Maybe. Maybe not. Sometimes big fish under the small ones, sometimes not.' He kept the bow pointed resolutely shorewards.

'Let's have a look,' said the boy.

'It's getting late,' said the serang. The boy looked at his watch.

'Three. Plenty of time. Sunset's only at seven. Let's go.'

He was determined and he had hired the boat. The serang swung her around and opened the throttle so that the little engine clattered at maximum revolutions and they crawled towards the distant white specks.

The birds were small white terns diving on a scattered sardine shoal. They trolled back and forth for an hour without getting a strike and the boy's frustration sat in his stomach like a dull pain.

'Let's go,' he said finally. 'What a bloody day.' His face was burning and he felt the yawning advent of seasickness. The fish they had caught lay flat-eyed, grey and stiff, on the sun-baked boards.

They turned towards the invisible coast and after a mile the engine stopped without any warning. It was very quiet in the boat for a full minute while the way fell off and *Poor Man's Friend* lay without moving on the oily sea.

The serang cleaned the plugs and checked the ignition and swung the handle and the exhaust bubbled weakly into the sea but the engine did not fire.

When the serang was tired he sat down on the thwart and wiped his face.

'It never stop before,' he said, looking at the engine with reproach.

'Well, it bloody well has now,' said Faraday.

'You know anything about engines?' asked the serang.

'No.'

When the serang was rested he tried again. The boy sat watching him with growing anger, which ebbed to a faint anxiety as the afternoon faded and the engine remained silent.

2

Harry Koenig and his wife sat on the stoep of their small white cottage in the tourist camp and drank gin and tonic and watched the sea. He was a tall thin man, tanned and flat-bellied and very healthy-looking despite his drinking, which was heavy even for Johannesburg. His thin fair hair was brushed back in two wings over his big ears. His eyes were blue and only slightly veined and very direct. He was wearing clean khaki shorts, an expensive dark blue cotton shirt, and sandals. The strap of his Rolex Oyster showed very white against the dark skin of his forearm. He looked cool and relaxed and exactly what he was, a rich man slumming a holiday in a cheap tourist spot.

His wife sighed noisily, puffing out her cheeks. She was short and fat and quite unattractive. Her nose was long and very prominent and her eyes were flat and unfriendly most of the time and she sweated a lot in the heat. Now she had dark patches showing in the armpits of her expensive blue sundress and little globules of sweat glistened on her upper lip.

'I really can't take any more of this, Harry,' she said.

'It's the boy's last holiday,' he said, looking out to sea. He looked at his watch. 'Time they got in. Guess they must have hit the fish, all right.'

'Harry.'

'Yes, dear.'

'Did you hear what I said? I'm not staying here another day. Not another bloody day. You must speak to Farrie.'

'Farrie heard they were getting a run of katonkel here,' he said.

'And you had to drag me along.'

'About time we had a family holiday,' he said.

'In this god-forsaken hole? Why the hell didn't we go to Beira or Paradise Island or somewhere?'

Koenig sighed. 'Because Farrie heard they were getting the katonkel here. I told you.'

'Christ, but I'm tired of fishing,' she said. 'I wish he'd take up something else.'

She lay back in the deck chair and shut her eyes. Koenig sat looking at her and trying to remember how he had once felt about her. How the hell, he thought bitterly, how the bloody hell can people change so much? Not only physically. I could stand that. He looked at the sweaty pudgy woman opposite him and felt dull resentment. Coldly he surveyed her, feature by feature, dwelling for several seconds on the thin petulant mouth which never seemed to open these days except to nag, chide, whine, complain or coarsely berate. She was coarse, physically and mentally. Twenty years ago she had seemed charmingly, endearingly outspoken; now she revolted him with her insensitivity. Marriage had addled her personality. She was still the girl he had married – almost. But the flippancy had become shallowness, the pleading voice had become a whine, the pouting mouth a symbol of perpetual petulance; and the small neat body had become encysted in the fat of middle age: girdled, painted, powdered, dyed, coiffeured and incredibly gross.

She opened her eyes suddenly and he looked away with a guilty start, pretending to be absorbed in the dusty road between the cottages where the big Lincoln Continental stood among the battered pre-war Fords and Chevs. The road wound down towards the harbour through a clump of Port Jackson willows with their pale grey trunks and small drab green leaves. The ground under them was a brown carpet of fallen leaves.

They were having their twentieth anniversary in the autumn. Twenty years. He sat and thought about that. They had not been twenty happy years, or even twenty friendly years. They had most certainly not been twenty faithful years. He had had a long line of affairs – how he hated that word, with all its purse-lipped suburban disapproval.

Some of them, most of them, had been fairly dreadful, debasing to a greater or lesser degree. Harry Koenig knew this. He did not like it but he was a man and he could see no other way out. Thelma would not give him a divorce: she was living very well and wanted to keep it that way, thank you very much. Nor would she ever give him grounds for divorce, he knew. Oh, my wife is most faithful, he thought. Most faithful. She would never look at another man. Thelma did not need men, or affection, or love, or lust. All she wanted was her talented children, her beautiful home, her servants, her bridge club, her chairmanship of the local branch of the N.C.W., her membership of the Rotary Anns, her assured position in Johannesburg society.

Some of Harry's affairs had been almost happy, with the strange masochistic happiness of what is called illicit love: they had been the worst.

He had come back sometimes and tried to make things work. He had tried to explain to Thelma what he needed. She never could understand him. Bed was a sacrificial altar to her. My wife, he had said, fumblingly, my wife, you are killing me with this oh-very-well-here-it-is-now-take-it-and-don't worry-Mummy-again attitude. But she stared at him blankly, uncomprehendingly, her eyes empty of any understanding, or, worse, any desire to understand.

So he had become the Misunderstood Husband. He sat on the stoep and thought about it. He did not like it at all. He didn't like the deceit and the glances from waiters and hotel-keepers and the sly smiles of many of the girls themselves. But he knew it would go on. There was somebody he had to call in Port Elizabeth, and he knew he would: next week he would drive up. He could plead a business deal. Thelma knew he was lying, and she knew he knew she knew, but they kept up the fiction. It was part of the hypocrisy which entangled them.

He sat on the stoep and looked at the darkening sea and felt terribly depressed.

His wife heaved herself upright and the deck chair squeaked.

'Johnson!' she called. Her voice was piercing in the still afternoon. The cook-boy shuffled out on to the porch.

'Yes mam?'

'You can lay the table. We won't wait for Baas Faraday.'

'Yes mam,' he said. He went back into the darkness of the cottage and they heard the sounds of the table being laid. It was getting dark and Johnson brought out the mantle-lamp and its hard white light made a bright pool on the grass in front of the stoep. They sat watching the road between the trees until there was no more light to see by and then they went inside and ate. Afterwards they came back on to the stoep and sat without speaking. The night was very still. They could hear the sea a long way off, and in one of the other cottages somebody was playing a radio too loudly, but these sounds only emphasised the stillness of the night around the camp.

At ten Harry Koenig stood up and walked heavily down the wooden stairs and on to the dusty road. His wife watched him go without speaking. He walked along the road, feeling the heat of the day radiating from the powdery surface, and through the clump of willows to the harbour. There were lights and noise there, and the shadowy shapes of men bustling

31

around the single derrick which was used to swing fish-baskets from the boats.

He walked faster, composing under his breath the rapping he would give the old Malay, and later, in the cottage, Faraday. He walked quickly and purposefully and when he reached the quay he was quite angry, at himself for becoming anxious and at his son and the coolie for putting him in such a position.

But when he reached the light he saw that his son was not there. He walked to the edge of the quay and looked down into the black and glistening harbour and saw the gap in the line of moored boats. He felt his anxiety come back in a sudden wave.

He turned back to the men under the light. There were five or six of them. Coloureds and Malays, glittering with fish scales and grubby in their torn and dirty clothes. They looked at him without curiosity and went on with the unloading. Small fish, mackerel, maasbanker, and elft, lay in glittering piles on the jetty.

'Where's that boat?' he asked, pointing to the line of boats at the perimeter of the light. They stopped working and looked at him as though they had not seen him before. One of them touched his dirty beret self-consciously.

'The *Friend*? Master means the *Friend*, Master?' he spoke with the slurred whine which in the Cape Coloureds is some-times funny and sometimes irritating. Koenig felt anger stir in his stomach.

'The old man's boat,' he said. They smiled and nodded as though a great truth dawned.

'Yes,' he said, trying to hold his temper. 'Yes. The old man's boat.'

'Plenty elft tonight, master,' said one of the fishermen. He pointed to the fish on the quay, shining in the hard electric light. 'Plenty elft. Perhaps he stay out to catch more.'

Koenig thanked them and walked back to the cottage. When he got there the stoep was empty and all the lights were out. He felt his way inside, swearing at the dark, and groped towards his bed. He heard springs creak as his wife's heavy body stirred.

'Harry? Harry?' her voice was thick with sleep.

'Yes,' he said. 'It's me.' He sat on the bed and slipped off his sandals.

'Farrie?'

'Not back yet.'

The bed-springs gave a sudden shriek as she sat up. He heard her fumbling on the table for the matches.

'What? Not back? Harry –'

He walked bare-footed across the floor and groped around until he found the matches. He lit one and took off the still warm glass chimney of the small lamp and lit the wick. It flared yellow with a tail of smoke and he turned it down and replaced the chimney. Thelma was wearing a pink flounced nightdress. She lit a cigarette by holding it over the top of the lamp and took a long draw.

'I've been down to the harbour,' said Koenig. 'The other boats have just come back. They think the coolie's stayed out late because the fish are biting.'

'But it's so late, Harry!'

'I know. It's bloody inconsiderate of him.'

'I wouldn't worry if he was out with anyone we know, in a big boat or something, but just that little boat and that old coolie.'

'I know,' said Koenig. 'I know. But it's no bloody use getting into a sweat about it.'

'Harry, we're going home tomorrow. First thing. I'm not staying here another day. Not another day, not one.'

'All right, Thelma. All right. But for God's sake don't let's harp on about it all night. The boy's late and that's all there is to it.'

'If that's all you care when your son –'

'For heaven's sake, Thelma.'

She stubbed her cigarette with vicious stabs and turned over in bed, pulling the blankets around her shoulders, so that all he could see of her was the ludicrous cactus of her dark yellow hair, wrenched into tight bunches by the plastic jaws of the overnight curlers. He sat watching her for a few seconds and noticed that her hair was almost brown at the roots. Back to the old bottle, he thought. Dye today blonde tomorrow. He went through to the small bathroom and brushed his teeth and washed his face. He stood looking out of the window for several minutes, thinking about his son. He sighed and went back to the bedroom and slipped out of his shirt and shorts, hanging them over a chair. He got into bed without putting on his pyjamas and lay on his back with his arms down his side. It was very quiet. Through the window he could see the dark bulk of the mountain behind the cottage and a narrow strip of star-flecked sky. He heard his wife turn restlessly and he felt a sudden sympathy for her.

'Go to sleep, Thellie,' he said. It was the first time he had called her Thellie for many years.

'I'm worried,' she said in the dark.

'There's nothing to worry about,' he said. 'They'll be back any time now.'

But he lay awake most of the night, and when he woke in the grey of the morning his son had not come home.

*   *   *

When night came it grew colder on the water. The serang made a small tent out of the brown sail and they sat under it, watching the stars dip and sway with the motion of the boat. They sat without speaking. The boy was furiously angry. There was no fear yet, just anger that he should be put in this position. He thought of his father's irritation and his mother's tearful recriminations when they did finally get home. What a dockside scene there's going to be, he thought, wincing. He had all youth's horror of scenes of any sort.

But behind the wall of his anger he was already composing the story for his friends. This old coolie balled things up, see, went all to pieces, and what a job I had, man, you can't imagine, drifting southwards in this little tub – an unpleasant thought intruded.

'How far out do you think we are?' he said.

'Maybe twenty miles, bit more, bit less,' said the old man.

'Oh,' said Faraday. Twenty miles suddenly seemed very far indeed.

'Coffee?' asked Pillay.

'Yes,' said the boy, subdued by the thought of those twenty miles.

Pillay went forward and lit the small brazier, crouching on the floorboards and blowing. When it was drawing he balanced his billycan on the top and sat there holding it while it heated. The boy came and sat on the thwart beside the brazier, shivering a little.

They drank the coffee from two small tin mugs, made from jam-tins with strip handles riveted to the sides and sat beside the dying fire.

To the north-east a light glowed just below the horizon, flared redly and faded.

'What's that?' said the boy, pointing. 'There – now it's gone.'

'Cape St Francis Lighthouse. Long way from us.'

'Can't we send up a flare – have you got flares?'

'I got flares. No good sending him up for St Francis, though. They not see us. That light too far away.'

'Oh,' said the boy, disappointed.

'Better we keep the flares till we see a ship near,' said the serang.

'Yes,' said Faraday. He sat watching the flare and fade of the light.

'I think we should use a flare,' he said. He stood up, swaying slightly as the boat moved.

'Where are they?' The serang sat silent beside the red and black ashes of the brazier, looking at him. Then he got up and went aft and opened the stern locker. He pulled out a large square tin and prised off the lid. The boy watched him. The serang took out the small hand-flare and brought it back.

'We got others?' asked Faraday. The serang nodded. The boy looked at the far-off light again. It seemed much weaker, just a red pulse on the horizon.

Faraday stood on the gunwale and hooked one arm around the stay. He held the flare out and ripped the igniter. The flare hissed in a low arc across the darkness and fell into the sea fifty yards away. Faraday jumped back into the boat.

'Is that all – that as high as it goes?'

'Only a small flare,' said the serang.

'We need a rocket,' said Faraday. He sat down on the thwart again and watched the faint intermittent glow of the lighthouse. He suddenly felt like crying. There was a slight breeze from the invisible land now, chopping at the water.

The old man felt the wind and thought: now we must do something or we will have drifted so far by morning that they will never find us. He looked over the side and saw from the faint phosphorescent turbulence that the boat was moving. Already, he knew, they were drifting at a knot or two, caught in the wide south-flowing current.

Now, with a wind pushing them, they would make a half-knot more: enough to move them fifteen miles by daybreak. He got up and unlashed the brown sail, feeling the stiff canvas crackle under his hands. He unclipped the hoist from the port stay and shackled it to the gaff and heaved down on the hoist. The sail lifted, swaying and cracking in the wind, and he left the foot flapping until he had heaved the gaff home and secured the lower end so that the gaff lay at an acute angle to the stubby mast. Then he took the sheets and rove them through the fairleads in the gunwales. The boy sat watching him, his anger showing on his face.

The serang took the port lead and went aft again, sitting in the stern sheets and taking the tiller. When he hauled in the lead the sail bellied and he hauled the lead in hard and he felt the boat move as the sail filled. He pushed over the tiller to bring her up into the wind and the boat began moving forward, heeling slightly, with the slopping of the sea around her changing to a swift trickling as she picked up speed.

Now if we had a keel, thought the serang, a deep keel like the racing yachts that come up from the Cape, we could sail right into this beautiful wind, and sail ourselves home. But we have no keel, and although we seem to be going ahead very nicely, sailing like a yacht, we are going sideways at the same time, and very little forwards; just enough to hold us where we are, and stop the wind blowing us further out to sea. He looked at the boy, who was smiling now, although he was trying not to show it, and he felt suddenly sorry for him.

'Man, we're moving!' said Faraday. 'We should have done this before.' He had temporarily forgotten his anger.

And all the time, thought the serang, the big wide deep current has us in his arms and takes us south. He was not very worried yet. I don't have to worry, he told himself, they will come looking for me. I have a rich white boy aboard. When he had admitted this to himself he felt suddenly angry and ashamed. He pulled the rope tighter around his hand and sat watching the swaying stars. The Southern Cross was dead ahead.

The wind coming on the beam was cold and the spray which spattered inboard was icy. That's the south-easter, thought Pillay. Always it makes the sea colder. Sometimes when the south-easter had blown on this coast he had known the water to chill so rapidly that thousands of fish died, floundering in dying masses in the shallows in a desperate search for warmer water.

He had put on his shirt and was going to pull on his jersey

when he saw that Faraday was shivering. He held out the jersey to the boy.

'Want this, Boss?' The boy shook his head.

'No. I'm okay.' He sat on the floorboards of the boat, sheltering in the lee of the gunwale, clutching his arms around his legs and resting his head on his knees, pulling his body into as small a space as he could.

He was miserably cold and spray had collected on his face and hair and trickled down his neck so that his shirt was wet and sticking to him. He tried to fall asleep but the movement of the boat and the intermittent showers of spray would not let him. He wished he had taken the serang's jersey.

He had refused automatically. He had the natural repugnance of a white to wearing a non-white's clothes. He had gone to school in the Transvaal. One morning, when he was still at primary school, the principal called a special assembly to disclose a shocking thing: a black child had been found wearing a cast-off school blazer.

He held out, skewered on a garden fork, the offending garment, and delivered a five-minute homily on the necessity of never, never, never, not for the sake of charity or anything else, letting the school blazer be so debased.

Then the children were marched outside and grouped in a solemn hollow square in the hot Transvaal morning while the principal ceremoniously burned the soiled blazer.

It was an impressive demonstration, and one which left a solid thumbprint in the five hundred young minds assembled in the school quadrangle.

So now, a decade later, Faraday Koenig wrapped his arms around his damp body and shivered and remembered sunlight, aching bright, on the white walls of the school, and the somnolent buzzing of bees in the slow-rustling gums around the quadrangle. He closed his eyes and saw the frieze of serious child faces and smelt again the acrid wispy smoke of the burning blazer and felt the warmth lap his body.

Towards dawn the wind dropped and the boat wallowed uncomfortably in a short confused sea. Pillay left the tiller and lit the brazier and they warmed and drank the rest of the coffee and grilled the smallest katonkel on the coals. The sun came up while they were eating and they felt the first soft breath of the west wind.

He looked at the pale sky and the very high clouds and thought, I hope it doesn't come through from the west today. The moon is full in two days and the spring tide swell will be building up and with a westerly we will have a big sea.

The boat was rolling heavily now, sliding down into the troughs and lurching slowly up on the following swell. The sail snapped and cracked uselessly. Pillay lowered the gaff and stowed the sail and then struck the mast, lashing it lengthways in the boat. After this the boat did not roll so badly. Then he sat down in the stern sheets and looked at the boy.

'Don't worry, Boss,' he said. 'They come looking for us this morning. Don't worry.'

'I'm not worried,' said Faraday. His eyes were prickling with tiredness and there was a flat stale taste in his mouth. He scooped up some seawater and tried rinsing his mouth out, but it did not make much difference. A thought struck him.

'Have we got water?'

Pillay pointed to a green oil tin lashed under the midships thwart. Faraday unscrewed the lid and saw that it was full.

He put his face down and smelled it. The can had not been cleaned properly and there was still the smell of oil. Suddenly he felt very afraid.

Later in the morning they tried to start the engine. On the thirtieth swing the starting handle key sheared. Pillay sat down suddenly with the useless handle dangling from his fingers and swore at the silent engine. He swore long and very fluently and the boy looked at him with something approaching awe.

3

Blunt, the harbour-master at Bloubaai, was a conscientious man, attaching as much importance to the arrivals and departures of the little fishing boats as his counterparts in the big ports did to the ocean liners.

When *Poor Man's Friend* had not returned by sundown, he noted it in his log, but he was not alarmed. Beyond the dusty windows of his small office the sea gleamed faintly, flat and tranquil.

He looked at the barometer and studied the weather reports again. The mercury stayed high and the forecast promised a light south-easter. Nothing to worry about. He switched off the lights and went out, locking the door behind him.

He walked out of the harbour and up through the quiet town to his house. His wife was sitting on the porch. He kissed her and they sat watching the sea until it was time to go in for dinner.

They could see the whole sweep of the bay and the black mass of the high mountains to the east. The moon was up and the sea sparkled.

Before he went to bed he came out and stood on the porch again and looked at the sea for a long time. Then, partly satisfied, he went to bed. He lay awake for a long time, listening to the far-off sound of the sea. It was after midnight before he fell asleep.

Blunt slept very badly. Long before dawn he was awake, and wondering what had awakened him. He lay in bed and smoked a cigarette and then he heard the dog again, faint, unhappy howling drifting across the shallow valley which separated the fishermen's huts from the rest of the village.

'Bloody hound,' he thought, and then remembered Pillay. He got out of bed and walked to the window. From his house he could see the harbour. It lay like a moonlit pond before him, ruffled slightly by the south-east breeze. He saw the gap in the line of moored boats and swore softly. From the darkened room behind him his wife spoke:

'Is the *Friend* back yet?'

'No.' He looked down at the boats again and then out at the black and silver sea.

'It's not like him to stay out without warning you,' said his wife.

'No. But perhaps they hit a big shoal.'

'Did the other boats?'

'No. Nothing unusual. Plenty of elft, that's all.'

'He wouldn't stay out all night for elft,' said his wife.

The dog howled again.

'His dog,' said Blunt's wife.

'Yes.'

His wife got out of bed.

'I'll make some coffee,' she said. 'You'll be going down early?'

'Yes.'

They sat on their beds and drank the coffee and watched it grow lighter outside.

Blunt dressed and walked out into the morning. It was still cool and he could smell the dew and the damp earth. He walked over the hill to the fishermen's cottages. He could hear the dog howling again.

It was very quiet. His feet made no sound on the dusty road. Over this side of the hill it was hot already. The air was heavy and still.

The pale willows sagged tiredly beside the road. Scraggy hens clucked and scratched in the dirt. There was a faint smell of rotting fish.

Pillay's cottage was at the end of the road. It was fresh-painted, white with blue window frames and a blue door.

There were faded net curtains at the two small windows. The small garden was neat and well-tended. There were carrots and potatoes in the front beds and in the side beds there were the vivid orange splashes of pumpkin-flowers. The beds were bordered with white-washed stones.

The dog was sitting on the front door-step, howling and scratching at the door. When it saw Blunt it ran to the fence, barking and wagging its tail. It knew him well.

Blunt let himself in and tried the front door to the cottage.

It was unlocked. He and the dog went inside. It was dark inside after the early morning sunlight.

Blunt poured the dog a dish of water and found some stale bread. The dog ate it hungrily, his jaws snapping as he gulped.

The inside of the cottage was as neat as the outside. In the main room there was a scrubbed table, two chairs, a small old radio on a box near the window. On the walls were tacked hunting and fishing prints from *Esquire* magazine. The floor was of unstained planks, white with scrubbing.

When the dog had finished eating and drinking, Blunt went out, closing the door behind him. He let the dog out into the road and closed the gate.

The dog looked uncertainly from him to the house, as though making up its mind.

Then it ran ahead of him down to the harbour. When he got there the dog was running eagerly among the men getting ready to go out that morning, sniffing at them, looking up at their faces.

When it realised Pillay was not among them it sat on the wall and looked out to sea.

Blunt went into his office and opened the windows. He filled the kettle with fresh water and got out the coffee-pot.

Through the window he could see the dog sitting on the wall.

*   *   *

Harry Koenig slid quietly out of bed and walked through to Faraday's room. He knew before he switched on the light

44

that his son had not come back. He let himself out on to the verandah and stood looking at the sea.

The sky was deep blue overhead, paling in the east and the morning air was cool.

Birds were chirping sleepily in the willows and down among the fishermen's huts a dog was howling. The low mutter of the surf came up from the beach.

He went back inside and got dressed in slacks and a jersey, pulling them on in the dark so as not to waken his wife, and then went out silently, walking swiftly down the dusty road to the harbour.

Other figures were moving through the small town now: there was the low murmur of voices, the soft clinking of billycans, a steady shuffling of feet, and the soft bubbling of exhausts from the harbour. The boats were getting ready for sea.

He walked along the quay towards the harbour office. Through the seaward window a pale light gleamed.

Koenig clumped heavily up the stairs and pushed open the door. Blunt was sitting at his desk, looking as though he had just got up.

There was a pot on a hotplate behind him and the smell of coffee was fresh on the morning air.

'Sit down, Mr Koenig,' said Blunt. 'Cup of coffee?'

'Please.'

Blunt poured the coffee into thick white china cups, added milk and sugar at Koenig's nod, and pushed one across the desk at him.

'Thanks.'

'I guess you've been pretty worried, Mr Koenig?'

'Naturally.'

'They didn't say anything about staying out all night?'

'No. Not to me. I'll kick his bottom when they get in.'

'Well, it's up to the skipper, you know.'

'My son's pretty stubborn. I don't think they'd have kept out so long unless Farrie wanted to.'

'Well,' said Blunt, 'I don't think there's anything to worry about yet. There was a light south-easter during the night, about ten miles an hour, nothing to worry about. If they're not in by eight, I'll ask Mossel Bay to send a tug along the coast. There's lots of bays and headlands they could get behind.'

'A tug?' said Koenig. 'That's causing a lot of trouble, isn't it?'

'It is,' said Blunt. 'I'd send our big launch out, but it's up on the slip. Anyway, I've also asked the boats that are going out today to keep their eyes open. But I reckon that they're probably anchored inshore somewhere. Particularly with that wind last night. That comes along the coast, and Pillay would have swung inshore to get in the lee of the hills, rather than buck right into it. His boat's very wet. Makes a lot of water in a head sea . . .'

Through the dusty window they saw the first of the boats slip seawards, blue circles jetting from its tall thin smokestack. Faintly they heard the pop-op-op-op of its engine. The fishermen were sitting in the stern.

They all wore yellow sou'westers and they were very bright against the grey sea and the black boat.

One of them waved as the boat passed the signal station. Then the boat turned around the end of the wall and they could not see the men in their yellow sou'westers any more.

Two more boats came out together. They could hear the crews shouting to each other. It was now fully daylight and the first sun was in the office, making it seem dustier than before.

Blunt looked at Koenig and saw the tiredness and worry etched into his face and he felt sorry for the man, despite his money, and he never felt sorry for anyone with money as a rule, it being his private and very firm belief that money could buy everything.

But he looked at Harry Koenig and saw the full eyes and the faint twitch in the left lid and he felt sorry for him.

He opened his mouth to make some comforting platitude when the telex machine on the table behind him gave a warning beep-beep, clicked a few times, and started to chatter a message. Blunt leaned back and tore off the strip of paper as it emerged. He felt Koenig's fear reach across the desk to him as he read it. He picked up the telephone and thumbed the rest to attract the exchange, pushing the message across to Koenig.

Koenig read it slowly, pushing down the fear which was bubbling in the back of his throat like vomit.

It read:

WEATHER REPORT FOR PERIOD ENDING NOON DECEMBER 7. COASTAL BELT, PLETTENBERG BAY TO PORT ST JOHNS: WINDS LIGHT TO VARIABLE BECOMING STRONG TO GALE FORCE LATER SCATTERED SHOWERS . . .

He dropped the paper on the scarred wood and stared at Blunt, realising that this was the port captain's field, that there was nothing he could do, no suggestion he could make.

Blunt was speaking urgently, rapidly, to Mossel Bay. He had pulled a naval survey map of the area out of a drawer and was tracing the coast line with his finger as he spoke. When Blunt had finished he swivelled around in his chair and looked at Koenig. He picked up the weather report and looked at it again, and then looked at the wall clock. It was six-ten.

'If it's going to blow,' he said, 'it'll start coming through about mid-morning.'

'How bad will it be?' asked Koenig.

'Gale, they say. They're not always right, you know, Mr Koenig. But I'm not taking a chance. I've asked the port captain at Mossel Bay to have his tug stand by.'

'I'm sorry about this,' said Koenig.

'Not your fault,' said Blunt. Through the window he saw the last of the boats slip through the gap. 'I've got to put the warning up,' he said. 'You go and get some breakfast and perhaps I'll have something for you in an hour or two. I've asked Mossel Bay to keep in touch.'

When Koenig had gone Blunt climbed the ladder to the top of the tower and hoisted the black gale-warning cones. The light south-easter had dropped and the air was very still. The last boat was only a hundred yards out and, looking back, the crew saw the black cones and waved.

Blunt knew they would pass on the warning and felt relieved. He climbed back down the ladder and poured himself another cup of coffee.

He sipped it slowly and hoped the westerly held off until late in the day. A summer westerly on that coast could be a very bad thing.

48

He picked up his binoculars and went up to the tower again. He rested his elbows on the parapet, white with gull-droppings, and swept the sea very carefully. He saw, and was glad to see it, that the boats had kept close inshore. They were anchored off the redfish grounds, a few miles from the harbour. At least I don't have to worry about them, he thought. It was hot on the tower and he felt sweat forming in his armpits and along the band of his cap and the lenses of the glasses began to fog. The sky was a bright hard blue except in the west, where it was grey over the mountains. Overhead there were a few very high thin clouds.

Koenig came back at nine and they stood in silence in the hot tower, watching the sea. The first light breath of the westerly fluttered on the water. Blunt turned the glasses inland and looked at the hills. Through the glasses he could see the red dust clouds whipped from the roads.

'Here it comes,' he said. Then they could feel it on their faces.

Blunt lifted the glasses once more, without hope. They went down into the stuffy office and Blunt called Mossel Bay while Koenig looked helplessly at the chart, with its whorls and lines and dots and speckles which were meaningless to him.

Blunt replaced the telephone.

'The tug's leaving now,' he said.

Koenig stood up.

'I'd better tell my wife,' he said. 'Thank you very much. Will you let me know – ?'

'Yes. The tug will keep in touch. Anything comes through, we'll let you know.'

'I'll come back down here,' said Koenig. 'I'd like to be here. You won't mind?'

'No. You come back here if you like. But don't worry. The tug'll pick them up. Just don't worry. There's no danger yet.'

'I am worrying,' said Koenig. 'I am bloody worried.' He went out and walked up the dusty road to the cottage.

Thelma's face screwed up when he told her. For God's sake don't throw your hysterics now, he thought. Please don't hide yourself from this like you have all our other little tragedies.

Because this may be a big tragedy for us, and I don't want to carry it all alone, and I especially don't want to bear it alone for both of us while you withdraw into your own private storm-shelter until it's all over.

'Please,' he said, and she looked at him as though he were a stranger.

He left her sitting in the sun on the verandah and went inside and showered and shaved and Johnson fried him some eggs and bacon.

He put on a clean shirt and shorts. When he came out again she was still sitting there. She had a glass in her hand and the brandy bottle was standing on the concrete beside her chair. The morning sunlight filtered through the brandy and made a golden puddle on the rough concrete.

'Bit early, Thelma,' he said. He was being very tactful and careful not to upset her.

'I need it,' she said. 'You don't know what this has done to me.' She took a drink. When she lowered the glass there was a red smudge on the rim.

'I blame this all on you, Harry. All of it. I hold you personally responsible.'

'He's my son too, Thelma,' he said. 'I'm just as worried.'

'You should never have agreed to come to this dreadful place. Never. Why didn't you put your foot down?'

Because I've never put my foot down, he thought. I've always taken the easy way out. Perhaps I've felt guilty, felt that I've spent more time on my business than on my family. So I've always given in. Like now.

In the still air under the corrugated-iron roof he could smell the aromatic liquor and it made him feel nauseous.

He had never liked drinking early in the day. He sat down beside her and tried not to worry.

It was very hot and now the rising wind was eddying around the verandah. It was beginning to scoot dust and leaves along the road.

Somewhere a willow-branch was scraping on an iron roof, a monotonous, nerve-grating scree-scraw. He could see the ocean through the grey boles of the willows. It had lost its blue colour and was a dirty tumbled grey-green. The wind made a low whistle around the telephone wires.

'Why don't you have a drink?' said his wife.

'No thanks. I really don't feel like one.' Strange, he thought, how polite we are to each other. We really are most civilised creatures.

He stood up.

'I'm going down to the harbour again,' he said. 'They might have heard something. Coming?'

She shook her head.

'No. It will upset me. Will you come straight back if there is any news?'

'Yes.' He walked down the sun-warped wooden stairs and opened the gate into the road. When he reached the corner he looked back. His wife was pouring another drink. She waved vaguely. He turned and walked through the trees. The wind was stronger now and the branches overhead were creaking and the wind made a dry rushing sound in the leaves. It was ten-twenty.

4

When the wind settled Pillay stepped the mast again. The boy sat sullenly watching him, without offering to help. Stupid coolie bastard, he thought.

It's his bloody boat, and it's because of his bloody boat that we're stuck here and so he can work it himself. He sat with anger dull and heavy in his stomach, watching Pillay step the short mast and tighten the bottle screws on the stays. When the mast was stepped he hoisted the sail again and the boat began moving through the water. The steady heel and regular pitching were welcome after the formless roll and pitch.

The wind steadied and they heeled more, shipping spray.

There was a big swell and they chased across it at four or five knots, rising high on the smooth crests which were not yet broken by the wind.

Now that they were moving again the boy felt his anger ebbing. He moved aft and sat beside the serang. The old man was leaning well against the port gunwale, with the sheet rope doubled around his thick forearm.

He was sailing the boat very easily, giving her just enough rudder to hold her into the wind, or as high to windward as she would go, which was not very much. He hoped the wind would not increase, because then he would have to shorten sail or put on more rudder.

The boat handled badly under sail. She was not made for sailing. He looked at the silent engine and wondered why it had stopped. Something electrical, probably. Dirty points, maybe. He did not know much about engines.

He looked at the two long oars lashed from bow to stern and thought that he should have started rowing as soon as the engine failed.

At least he would have been closer inshore when the wind came. Now they were a long way out and he knew the wind was going to come through very strongly.

It had that feel to it, as though it were building up for a big blow, a buster. He was frightened.

'We're going okay,' said Faraday. 'We're going okay.' It was the first time he had spoken since dawn. The serang looked at him and smiled and the boy almost smiled back, but then he remembered his anger and stopped smiling.

There was a faint blonde adolescent stubble on his jaw and salt crystals glittered on his cheeks. He was very tired and wanted to sleep but the spray coming over the bow woke him every time he dozed. He sat there with his eyes shut and felt the sun on his face and the movement of the boat and swore when the spray stung him.

The sun and the movement evoked a drowsy sensuality in him, reminded him of sunny afternoons under the trees, sprawled in the long grass beside the cricket field, an afternoon compounded of the scent of crushed grass, the buzzing of bees, the dry stirring of leaves, the far off thok of bat against ball, slow eddies of clapping from the watching boys, the exciting glimpses of smooth brown legs from across the field, where a party of senior girls from the convent near by were watching the game ... over the tops of the trees he could see the school clock, hands transversing jerkily the gaps between the Roman numerals set in the white tower.

He dozed, and waited to be called. He felt no real interest in the game, or in whether his school won it or not, except inasmuch that victory by his team would reflect on him, and Faraday Koenig's pedestal would be jacked that much higher. He lay in the sun with his face on his new blazer, already smelling of chalk and ink and the indefinable aroma of the classroom, and looked at the girls giggling across the bright green, shadow-dappled grass ... he could see Con standing under the trees, tennis racket dangling from one hand. Long-legged, tanned, smart-talking Con. He stood up and started talking loudly, laughing with his head thrown back, hoping she would notice him, hoping that his turn to bat would come before she went home ...

Sudden spray lashed him across the face and shocked him awake. He felt tears of irritation in his eyes. The sun was hotter now and he began to feel nauseous again. Also he was hungry and thirsty. He crawled across to the water bottle and unlashed it and took a short drink. The oil-slick on the surface of the water made him retch.

He leaned over the side and heaved dryly. His diaphragm ached but nothing came up at first. Then there was the sudden bitter swill of bile in his mouth. He took another swallow of water and spat it out and felt better.

'Okay now?' asked the serang.

'A little,' he said. He sat down in the stern again. He had the disorientated feeling which comes from falling asleep in the sun. He closed his eyes and tried to think of home, but he couldn't bring back the picture.

The reality kept intruding now: the sun and wind and the feel of the salt dry on his skin. The movement of the boat, the creaking planking, the rushing sea.

Of course there would be a search for them. His certainty was partly the arrogance of the rich and partly the arrogance of the white. Already the planes are out, I'll bet, he thought. Or ships. He would prefer to be found by planes first. It was more dramatic. When I get back I'll write a letter to Con, he thought. He liked writing letters and thought he wrote them well.

Dear Con: A funny thing happened today ... he would keep it light-hearted, funny. She would probably have seen it in the newspapers by then. Play it cool, boy, play it cool. Oh you beautiful doll, he hummed.

... they were lying under the trees watching the game. Her school gym buttoned up the side, the first button starting nearly on the hip. She had long, very brown legs, firm from hockey and not yet muscular from swimming. The school gym was of cool light cotton, blue with a design of small white flowers, very neat. She looked very neat and fresh and a lot of brown leg was showing through the slit skirt. He was at the age when just to lie in the sun and look is enough.

He was taking her to the cinema that Saturday and he had made up his mind to kiss her. He had kissed girls before, in fact he was regarded as the school's Lothario, but he had never kissed Con Francis. She had direct green eyes, set very wide, and a sophisticated wit which put her above every other girl he knew and made him painfully reserved when he was with her, and that was unusual for him.

... he closed his eyes and tried to forget the sea but the noise and the movement kept intruding. Then he began to play a game with himself. I'll shut my eyes for half an hour at a time, he thought. That will make the day pass quicker. He screwed his eyes closed and sat very still and forced himself to think of other things.

He thought of school again but it was not summer any longer, it was winter, a bright hard June day with a thin wind like a knife across the muddy field and tattered strips of cloud low in the west. The boots of thirty boys drummed dully on the sodden pitch and splashed in the shallow puddles. There was a smell of sweat and wet grass and churned earth and a white vapour of breath hung over the panting scrum. There were a few cars parked under the trees, their windows steamed up, and every few minutes the occupants, parents, or masters off duty, would wipe them clean.

The scrum panted and heaved and broke, striped jerseys scattering like a break of quail and one was in the lead, running

56

crouched over the wet turf. In one of the cars somebody hooted and there was a spatter of shouts:

'Here, Farrie!'

'To me!'

'Keer hom!'

'Steek him!'

Smell of wet leather and feel of the hard ball and taste of sweat in one's mouth and the burning pain right under the ribs and only ten yards to go and then suddenly the way is wide open and unbelievably the line is crossed and he lies panting on the wet grass, feeling the mud on his face and still clutching the ball, curled around it protectively while the boys shout and the cars hoot under the trees and the whistle shrills again and again in the cold air.

In the changing rooms it is very hot and the showers hiss loudly in the cubicles against the far wall, and the air is thick with steam and sweat and liniment and the smoke of forbidden cigarettes.

The muddy jerseys lie in heaps on the puddled concrete floor. He sits quietly and dries himself. He is very brown, with just a small strip of white across his hips. The boys shake his hands and pat him on the back.

'Good show, Farrie, good show.'

'Fabulous, Farrie.'

'Stompie couldn't touch you.'

'You're in next year, for sure, Farrie.'

When he has showered and dried himself he dresses and smokes a cigarette and then walks out into the evening, closing the door of the shower room behind him. The wind has gone and the sun has set. The gravel crunches under his feet. He walks down the road behind the school, beneath the dripping pine trees, to where he has parked the car.

The head will not allow boys – even senior boys – to bring cars to school, so Faraday has to park his car where the head won't see it. It is not his car, it is his mother's, but she lends it to him most days. When he plays rugby on Saturdays he uses his father's car.

He is the only boy in the school who uses a car regularly. Some of the other seniors have little buzz-bikes, but none of them have cars.

He had taken his licence when he was sixteen. He had passed the test easily: he had been driving illegally since he was fourteen, sneaking his mother's car when she was sleeping in the hot summer afternoons, and taking his friends joyriding in the back streets.

He liked going to the drive-in cinema with the car. A gang of them would go most Saturday nights, boys and girls, wise-cracking and wrestling in the dark intimacy of the car, some-times glancing at the huge pictures seemingly hanging in the ink-blue sky.

It was strange that during this period of change, of the tasting of new pleasures, he should still have kept his interest in hunting and fishing. But he had. They were his first pleasures, introduced to him by his father, and their taste still lingered. His father had taken him fishing from the time he could walk, starting him with a bent pin in the rock-pools and graduating him through pool and gulley-fishing to the big tunny off Cape Point.

He dozed, and when he awoke they were still sliding across the swells.

The sun was behind dirty grey clouds and it was getting cold. The sea was shorter and steeper and the boat was moving much more. Faraday sat up and wiped the sleep from his eyes.

He had a bad headache now and the skin on his face felt as though it were about to tear. He looked at the waves. They were right on the beam now, coming in very fast and steeply and slamming the boat's bow off. Water was over the floorboards.

Pillay was sitting right on the gunwale, with one leg hooked under the thwart, and the other pushing the tiller hard over to keep the bow into the wind. The boat was crabbing badly. Her stern kept slewing. Pillay smiled when he saw that Faraday was awake.

'Come sit topside,' he said. 'We must keep her flat in the water.'

Faraday sat on the gunwale beside him.

'Where do you think we are?' he asked. The serang shook his head.

'*God weet*,' he said. Only God knows, he thought. He had been trying to work it out for hours. Now he was forced to admit that he knew only very vaguely where they were.

They were still a long way out, he knew, and far south of Bloubaai. He hoped one of the other boats had seen them turning out to sea again, towards the diving birds, and that the harbourmaster would guess they were in the current.

He did not like the sky. It promised a westerly buster. It also looked as though rain was coming. We are going to get it tonight, he thought.

This wind will not die at sunset. It will blow strong and wet all night and how I'm going to sail my boat in the dark I do not know, especially as I have only this rich man's son with me who knows nothing of the sea or boats and does not want to know anything.

He remembered the small tin-roofed church at Bloubaai and wondered if they had been prayed for yet.

No not yet, he decided. It was too soon. Tomorrow, if they were not home, Dominee Uys would hold a special service for the fishermen and they would pray for the safe return of *Poor Man's Friend*.

The idea embarrassed the serang. He never went to church, and he did not like the idea of being prayed for when he was in trouble. I never asked for nothing before, God, he said, and I don't want to start now. I got us into this and I'll get us out. No need for that Dominee Uys to come bothering you, God, no need at all.

He believed in God very much. He saw God in the sky and in the sun and in the mountains. He believed in Him and he felt sure that God was a very busy man, and not a man to be bothered with trivial things like a missing fishing boat. God's sure got bloody enough to do with those H-bombs and war rockets and things without them calling him up over me, he thought.

The wind rose with the sun and he had to spill the sail very often. Once he did not spill quickly enough and *Poor Man's Friend* heeled over and dipped her lee gunwale and shipped a lot of water.

'Hai,' said Pillay. 'We don't want any of that, *Friend*.' He tried to laugh it off so that the boy would not be worried, but the wind had taken him by surprise.

'Will you bale a little?' he asked Faraday. The boy was holding very tightly to the gunwale. The knuckles were showing white on the tanned hands.

'Jesus,' he said. 'I'm not a bloody skivvy. I paid to come on this bloody boat, you know.'

'Will you sail her, then?' asked Pillay.

'I don't know how she handles. Oh, bugger it, I'll bale.'

He sat on the thwart and worked the pump with short angry strokes.

'No good that way,' said Pillay. 'She won't suck like that. Long pulls.'

The boy looked away as though he had not heard, but he started using long steady strokes and soon the water was below the floorboards.

While he was on the thwart Pillay sailed the boat very easy. When Faraday had finished he came and sat on the gunwale again, blowing on his hands, and the serang hardened up again, pulling the sail in and trying to get the boat higher into the wind.

5

The two men sat in Blunt's office and watched the returning boats. It was nearly noon. Koenig sat in a chair at the window and looked at the harbour.

Behind the wall it was still calm, but the sea beyond the mouth was choppy and foam-flecked.

The wind beat against the window and droned around the radio aerials on the tower.

Blunt sat at his desk and wished the tug would radio. They had not heard anything from Mossel Bay for two hours. He listened to the wind and knew that a bad sea would be building up outside the bay.

He looked at his wall calendar. It was a gift calendar which showed the phases of the moon. Nearly spring tide. There was always a heavier swell with a spring tide.

They heard somebody coming slowly up the stairs. The door opened and Thelma stood in the opening with her hand on the jamb looking at them. Blunt stood up.

'My wife,' said Koenig. 'Thelma, Mr Blunt. Mr Blunt is the harbourmaster.'

Thelma walked into the room and Blunt pushed a chair out for her. She sat down. She had taken a lot of care with her dressing. She was wearing a yellow sundress and she had done her hair up and made up her face as though she were going out for the evening. In the hard sunlight coming through the window the make-up showed.

Her sandals were elaborate jewelled toe-strap affairs which she had bought in Venice.

She put her big Basuto-style sun hat on the desk in front of her and said:

'Well, Mr Blunt?' Koenig could see that she had been drinking. She spoke very carefully but he could detect the slight hesitation in her voice and he could see the liquor in her eyes.

62

'No news yet, Thelma,' he said, very quickly, appealing to her with his eyes to leave this to him and Blunt.

'There is a tug out, Mrs Koenig,' said Blunt.

'What good's a tug?' she asked. 'Tug. What good's a tug, I ask you?'

'As good as anything else,' said Blunt. What a bitch she looks, he thought. I'll bet she gives her husband a time. He was suddenly very grateful to his wife.

'Mr Blunt's doing everything he can,' said Koenig.

'Everything? Why don't you do something, Harry? We have some very good friends in the Government, Mr Blunt – Harry, who's that young man who works with Ben Schoeman, you know, the one who came out to Inanda with us?'

Oh you name-dropping bitch, thought Blunt. Oh you drunken name-dropping bitch. He smiled at Koenig to show that he was not offended.

'I don't think we need worry the Minister of Transport, Mrs Koenig. The Mossel Bay port captain has sent the tug out on his own authority. Mr Schoeman couldn't do more.'

'Please, Thelma,' said Harry. 'Let's leave it to Mr Blunt.'

'I just want to know that everything possible is being done,' she said. 'It's different for a mother. We feel these things more.'

'I'm sure they're all right,' said Blunt. 'Pillay is a very good skipper.'

'I don't know why Farrie wanted to go out in a tiny little boat with a decrepit coolie,' she said.

'I don't know.'

'We've been into all that, Thelma,' said Harry.

'When he wanted to come here, Mr Blunt, I said "Farrie, for God's sake why go to that God-forsaken spot when we can go anywhere else" – it was his last holiday, you see, before he goes to university, and his sister's in Switzerland, at finishing school in Lausanne, you know, and Harry and I cancelled our European trip this year because Lindy said she was going skiing with friends, and we decided to tour the country with Farrie, and now this has happened.'

'You're not very complimentary about Mr Blunt's town, Thellie,' said Harry, smiling apologetically.

'That's all right,' said Blunt. 'We're used to it.'

The telex chattered briefly and stopped. Blunt tore off the message. It was just a routine shipping movement. He skewered it on the wire spike on his desk and shook his head at Harry.

'Nothing. Just shipping advice.'

The hope ebbed from Harry's eyes.

'Oh.' He went back to his chair at the window. On the quayside three seagulls were fighting over a small dead fish. He sat watching them with absorbed interest. The waves were breaking against the sea wall and spray was blowing back into the harbour. The moored boats were nuzzling their buoys.

'Are we just going to sit here all day?' said Thelma.

'Well – ' said Harry.

'The tug should report any minute,' said Blunt. 'Why don't you and Mr Koenig go and have some lunch? If there's any news before you get back I'll send somebody up to your rondavel.'

'I couldn't eat,' said Thelma. 'I have no appetite, no appetite at all. I'm sure all this is terribly bad for me.'

'You must eat,' said Harry. 'Come on. Thank you, Mr Blunt.'

They walked down the stairs, Harry leading, and along the windy quay.

When they had gone Blunt pulled the chart out of his desk drawer again.

He marked with a pencil the tug's course and where he thought the *Friend* would be. He had pencilled small crosses in half a dozen small bays within twenty miles of Bloubaai. He was certain that Pillay, with engine trouble, perhaps, was waiting out the blow in one of these small bays. The coast was practically uninhabited along here, with Government forests running almost to the edge of the cliffs.

The radio crackled and he heard, through the rise and fall of static, Bloubaai being called. He picked up the handset and increased the volume.

'Bloubaai here.'

'Ah, Gerry – ' it was the tug.

'Luck, Bill? Over.'

The static whined and crackled.

' – Gerry, no, man. Sea's pretty wild out here. We're off Natspoeg now. Over.'

'Will you keep going? There's a chance they're in by the Sandwal. Over.'

'Righto. We'll go on up the coast far as Elands. But I think they're down, Gerry. Over.'

'Bad? Over.'

'Man, there's a nasty sea coming up. We're taking water all the time. Burning a lot of the taxpayer's fuel. Over.'

*   *   *

The pilot tug *Deneys Reitz* was not made for beating into a steep head sea. She sat low in the water and blundered right through each wave.

Bill Trout stood on the bridge and felt the spray sting his face and tried to dodge the solid water.

They were about five miles out. Inshore they could see the breakers surging up the high grey cliffs.

Two miles ahead the cliffs sloped down into a small low headland of yellow sandstone. This was the Sandwal. The soft rock had been undermined by the waves of centuries and had eroded into a series of spectacular blowholes. Through his glasses Trout could see the fifty-foot geysers erupt as each breaker heaved against the rock.

They came slowly and wetly abeam of the headland and the bay behind was empty.

'Damn,' said Trout.

It was calmer here and he rang down for more speed. The young second mate came up, wiping the spray from his binoculars.

'What do you think, Uncle Bill?' They were very informal aboard the Reitz. Trout shrugged.

'Not much hope.'

'Who's aboard?'

'One of Gerry Blunt's coolies and some kid from Johannesburg. His old man's a big noise, Gerry says.'

'I'll get some tea,' said the second.

Trout followed him into the shelter of the wheelhouse to light a cigarette. It was a relief to get out of the wind and spray.

The helmsman was a young man in a black jersey. He kept

both hands very lightly on the wheel and watched the sea ahead through the spinning Kent screen.

'How's she handling?' Trout asked him.

'Like a bitch, sir,' said the young man. 'Keeps falling off. Bit better now that we've speeded up, though.'

'Wait until we run before this,' said Trout.

'I'm waiting,' said the young man. 'And I'm laughing. My trick'll be over then.'

The second came back with two cups of tea and they stood and drank them in the wheelhouse. Trout finished his cigarette and they went out into the wind again. Sandwal was well astern and the coast was lifting into cliffs once more. There was a low cloud of spray all along the base of the cliffs.

They came to the big scar in the cliffs where the Elands River came down to the sea and there was still nothing ahead but wind-whipped sea. They had changed course slightly to follow the coast and now the wind and sea were on their quarter and the tug was harder to steer.

'I think they're out to sea,' said the second.

'I think they're down,' said Trout. 'In this sea.'

'Is Gerry Blunt sure they're along the coast?'

'That's his idea. He says the old man wouldn't have gone far out.'

'What about the south-easter yesterday?'

'Didn't blow hard enough or long enough to push them out.'

'I don't know,' said the second. 'On this coast, I just don't know.'

An hour later they turned back. Trout and the second stayed on the bridge. It was drier now that the sea was behind them. The wind came over the stern and blew the smoke down over the sea in a rolling grey cloud ahead of them. The sun shone through it red as a rising moon.

'We'll be in before dark,' said the second. He wiped moisture from his watch.

'I'd stay out all night if I knew where to look,' said Trout. He felt very bad about the trip. He felt that he had failed Blunt and the man and the boy he did not know.

'This is a hopeless coast,' said the second. 'Hopeless.'

Trout leaned against the bridge rail and remembered other boats which had gone missing. He tried to remember any which had been found. He could not think of any.

That was because boats only went missing when the weather was bad, and when the weather was bad on this coast no boat lasted long. So there was never such a thing as a hopeful search. Every search he had ever taken part in had been, like this one, a gesture.

He straightened up and the second said: 'Giving up?'

'Yes, I'll call up Bloubaai.'

He sat in the small warm wheelhouse holding the handset and watching the sea through the salt-streaked windows, waiting for Bloubaai to come through. Damn, he thought.

6

The wind shook the windows of Blunt's office. One of them was open slightly at the top and the wind stirred the sash cord, tapping it against the frame.

Koenig and his wife were back. Thelma had the dull eyes of an afternoon drinker. She exuded a faint smell of sour gin. Harry sat very stiffly on one of the hard Government-issue chairs, with his hands folded on his lap. He was trying very hard to stay calm.

Trout had just come through on the radio, and the words still floated in the stale air, drifting slowly to the floor. Nobody wanted to speak. They sat staring at the walls while the white-face clock jumped the seconds with a soft electric buzz.

From outside came the sound of the wind, the slapping of the sea, the rattle of spray on the wall.

When the wind faded there were the sounds of the town: a dog barking, whine of tyres on tarmac, the grind of a truck's gears in the main street.

Thelma began to cry. The tears ran straight down her face in two unbroken streams and collected on her chin.

They cut furrows through her make-up. Her hair came down as she sobbed and hung in crimped tendrils over her eyes.

Harry looked at her like a stranger for a moment, as though she were someone he had never seen before.

Then he jumped up and knocked his chair over and gave her his handkerchief. She was sobbing and talking quite incoherently. The damp make-up was smearing Harry's white handkerchief.

'Better take her home,' said Blunt. 'I've a lot to do here.' He made a vague gesture. 'Lot to get organised. Don't worry.'

Harry helped Thelma to her feet.

'For Christ's sake let's get organised. We've done nothing all bloody day. Please, let's do something.'

He went out with his wife and Blunt heard the Lincoln drive away. He sat down suddenly and rested his head on his hand and looked at the chart. He felt very tired and frustrated and quite helpless. While he was sitting there Harry came back. He sat down and said: 'I'm sorry about that.'

'She's upset,' said Blunt.

'No, I mean my going off pop,' said Harry.

'Oh, that,' said Blunt. He had forgotten. 'Oh. That's all right.'

'What I wanted to suggest,' said Harry, 'was couldn't you get in touch with Cape Town? I mean, have them send up a plane or a bigger ship? If it's any use, a good friend of mine is an MP. He'd hurry things – '

'I don't think we'd save any time, Mr Koenig. We're a long way from Cape Town.'

'Yes, but a plane – '

'Mr Koenig' – I'd better make things clear, thought Blunt. I'm not going to let this get out of control. It's my job, my area, my responsibility – 'this isn't the first time we've had a boat missing, you know. Leave it with us.' He noticed that he had taken to speaking of us rather than me. Was that, he wondered, because he was, in anticipation, shovelling some of the burden on to the shoulders of the amorphous they – the

70

Government, the lighthouse service, the Railways and Harbour Administration?

He turned to the radio.

'I'm putting out a call to all ships in the area, and to all lighthouses along the coast – '

'My wife's still in the car,' said Harry. 'I'll take her up to the cottage and come back.'

Thelma was sitting shapelessly in one corner of the wide seat. He started the engine and engaged the gears roughly and they drove out of the harbour. The lone customs officer waved idly from his cabin as they passed. In the town the wind was whistling around the buildings and blowing paper and leaves down the bare streets.

'I feel like a drink,' said Thelma.

'You've had enough already,' said Harry, but without any hope of convincing her. He did not feel like an argument. She opened her mouth to protest but he pulled the car into the kerb. There was an hotel across the street.

The hotel had double glass swing doors. Wallpaper had been pasted over the glass and the light which seeped through into the lounge was aqueous and depressing, like the light in an aquarium.

There were metal and plastic chairs and low, plastic-topped tables. In the corners of the room were dark green potted plants. They looked like starved rhododendrons.

A waiter without a jacket came across the dirty parquet flooring, scarred by thousands of cigarette stubs, and stood listlessly before them. Harry ordered a gin and tonic and a lager.

When the waiter had brought the drinks he did not leave

but stood a few tables away. They were the only people in the lounge.

The hush seemed to pervade the whole hotel. Once a telephone rang, briefly. It sounded far away.

'My pills,' said Thelma, suddenly. 'My pills. I won't be able to sleep tonight without my pills.'

He sighed and tried to keep his voice steady.

'Where are they? You had a bottle full when we arrived. Doctor Reay gave you enough for the holiday.'

She was scrabbling in her bag. He watched with dull irritation as she ladled the feminine debris on to the cheap table.

'I can't find them.' There was a touch of hysteria in her voice. She was a confirmed pill-taker; tranquillisers, stimulants, sleeping tablets, slimming pills, laxatives.

'They're not here,' she said. 'I'll never get a wink all night without them. I wonder if there's a chemist here – '

'They won't give them to you without a prescription,' he said wearily. Oh God. He was tired. The glass suddenly seemed very heavy in his hand. He put it back on the table too quickly, spilling some of the beer.

He watched the plump hands fumbling through the compacts and lipstick-soiled tissues and keys and coins.

There was a roll of notes, too: absently, he wondered what she was carrying so much money for. The waiter was watching her curiously. He saw Harry glance at him and looked away, flicking at a table with his cloth.

Thelma swept her things back into the bag and sat with it in her lap. Her lips twitched and he was afraid she was going to weep again.

'Thelma,' he said. He looked at the waiter and back at her.

The waiter was looking out of the window. He was humming softly.

'They will give them to me,' she said. 'They must. You'll explain that I must have them. Tell them who you are.'

'Wouldn't you like, just once, to go through a crisis by yourself, without leaning on something a chemist's contrived?' he asked, and was immediately sorry. She looked at him as though he had made an obscene noise.

'Harry. Harry, you can't mean that. I don't believe it. You know how I lie awake – '

'All right, Thelma,' he said. God, he was tired. He picked up the glass again and managed, by an effort of will which was painful in its intensity, to get it to his mouth without spilling any more beer.

'I'm having another drink,' she said, and by the way she made her mouth he could see what sort of afternoon it was going to be. Harry sat and nursed his beer. The room was warm and the beer was a tepid amber soapiness in a finger-marked glass.

7

By mid-afternoon sailing was very difficult. The wind was very strong now, coming in great wet blasts from the south-west.

Pillay sailed her very easily. He was just trying to keep her under way. It was harder to bring her up into the wind and sea. He was frightened that they would fall away and be broached.

They had taken a lot of water and the boy was on the pumps again. He had been on the pumps with hardly a break since noon and his hands were blistered.

The skin had broken over the blisters and the salt water made the raw places sting.

He worked the pump without looking at the serang or the sea, kneeling on the floor-boards with one arm hooked under the thwart to steady him. As he pumped he counted.

He was pretending that after a hundred strokes he would be able to stop. He had counted a great many hundred strokes and he had not yet stopped and the way he felt now he could go on all day and all night. Only his knees ached from kneeling on the boards and the arm clutching the thwart was cold. He shut his eyes as he pumped.

At first the spray had been irritating but now he did not notice it. He looked at his watch and was surprised to see that it was only four o'clock.

He stopped pumping and held it to his ear and was reassured when he heard it ticking. It was a good watch which his father had given him and he hoped the sea-water would not damage it.

'Hey,' said Pillay. 'Stop pumping now. You pump too much now. Give it a rest.'

'It's all right,' he said. 'I'm not tired.'

'Give it a rest,' said Pillay. The boy sat down on the boards and rested his head on his arms, leaning on the thwart.

Gradually the ache and the cold went out of his knees and arms and only his hands kept stinging.

'Like to try'n make the fire?' asked Pillay. He nodded and crawled forward to the brazier. The coals were black and wet.

He threw them overboard and started building up a new fire with small dry splinters from the underside of the thwarts and a scrap of paper from the locker.

The boat was moving so much now, with short, jerking lurches, that he had to work with one hand most of the time, holding on with the other.

He wedged himself between the engine housing the gunwale, and kept the brazier under the thwart to protect it from the spray while he laid the wood and paper. When he had found enough wood he got the matches out of the locker and lit the only piece of dry paper he could find, pushing it carefully in among the splinters of wood and blowing steadily until the flames caught.

It took a long time.

Some of the wood was wet and even though he sheltered the brazier with his body, spray kept coming over the side and hissing on the flames.

There was a lot of smoke from the damp wood and his eyes began to water. The smoke was thick and white.

It took a long time to get the fire burning well. When it was burning well he gutted the last katonkel and cut the fish into thick steaks, hacking through the backbone with the serang's big knife. The flesh was still quite firm.

He laid the steaks on the coals. When they had eaten they felt better. They kept two slices of fish for their next meal. And after that, I do not know, thought Pillay.

75

Then he looked at the torn and dirty sky and thought that perhaps they would not need any food, anyway.

He watched the boy eating his fish, licking the spiny rib-bones, and thought, I wonder what is in the boy's mind? Does he think this is my fault, or the fault of my boat, or does he blame himself a little? No, he would not blame himself. This sort of boy never blames himself. I wonder what his father and mother are doing now. The serang was suddenly glad that he had nobody ashore. It was enough to worry about himself. I need nothing else to worry me, he thought. For my own life I am worried enough already. I am really worried. I do not want to drown.

When he was young he had nearly drowned in Simonstown harbour. It had been unpleasant. After forty years he still remembered how unpleasant it had been.

Salt-water sits heavy in the stomach, heavier than fresh. Perhaps it would not be so bad to drown in fresh water.

In the war he had been on a minesweeper. They had picked up a great many dead bodies.

Sometimes it would be a boat full of desiccated corpses, sitting knee deep in green-scummed water, swaying with the roll of the boat.

Sometimes they would find seagulls screaming and wheeling over one lone corpse bobbing in a water-logged life-jacket.

They never found anybody alive in all those years. Now Pillay thought of the dead they had found and shivered a little. I am not so much afraid of dying, he thought. But I do not want to become one of those dreadful things we used to find, rotten, puffed and swollen like an *opblasie* fish, eyes picked out by seagulls. When I die I want to sink down into

76

the deep water, not float about until I am eaten by the birds.

The boy was sitting on the floorboards again. He had stopped pumping and it looked as though he was sleeping. His face was sullen in sleep.

The water was just above the boards. There was a lot of oil from the crankcase on the bilge-water and the oil-colours swirled in patterns with the motion of the boat.

The sun was very hot and coming straight down. He could feel it stinging his shoulders through his shirt. He was feeling tired again. He had felt tired earlier in the day but it had passed off. Now it was back and he knew that this time it was not going to pass. He could feel it pressing itself down on him, heavy as lead on his shoulders and thighs and arms so that he felt that he would never be able to move them again.

Never in his life had he wanted sleep so badly. He imagined himself walking up the dusty road to his cottage, feet shuffling in the dust, opening the gate, going up the white-washed path, opening the door, throwing himself on the bed. He would not even undress.

He would just lie down as he was, in his shirt and pants and boots, without taking anything off. There was something about just throwing yourself down like an animal and blunting the first sharp edge of sleep.

Later he would awake and wash and make coffee and then undress completely and get into bed properly, between the stiff white sheets, and this second time he would have time to lie there and listen to the wind and watch the sunlight coming through the curtains and let himself go gradually down the hill into sleep.

He would sleep all day and well into the night and awake

again in the early morning and lie there listening to the fishing boats leaving.

He would give himself a holiday that day. He would get up late in the morning and have breakfast and then walk down to the beach and talk to the octopus-catchers and then at midday he would go along to the bar and have a drink. And in the afternoon he would sleep again.

His head rolled suddenly to one side and he awoke with a nervous jerk. He leaned his head back and let spray splash over his face and run down his neck.

In the west the wind had stripped the clouds and the sun was low down. There was a pale yellow light on the waves. The foam which the wind whipped off was creamy and thick in the troughs of the waves.

The sea was running higher and more broken now and *Poor Man's Friend* was making no way at all.

She was just standing up into the wind and falling off, losing a lot of ground to the south-east. I cannot hold her much longer, thought the serang. This wind must drop with the sun. What about a sea-anchor? He had read of them, but he had never seen one used.

I don't think one would hold her into this sea, anyway. When I cannot use the sail any more I shall have to hold her head to the sea with the oars. The boy will help me. He will have to help me. He looked at the long oars lashed fore-and-aft and hoped he would not have to use them. You are an old man, he told himself. You cannot hold her through the night. Your heart will go. He turned his face into the wind.

'You bugger,' he said. 'Please stop now.'

8

Blunt sat and stared dully at the cross-marked chart on his desk and felt the confidence of the morning curdle in his stomach. Could he have been so wrong?

He had a headache. The office, with its door and windows shut to keep out the dust, was hot and airless. He wondered what he was going to tell Koenig. He looked at the clock: five. They would be back any time. The wind still beat about the buildings.

He turned to the radio and called Cape Town Radio. It took a few minutes to get through.

'I want an emergency call out,' he said, after identifying himself. 'To all ships, Cape St Francis to Cape Point: please keep lookout for small fishing boat with two men aboard.'

It was an admission of his error; and he felt no better after he had done it.

He heard the message repeated and then cut the contact. What next, he worried. What could he do. Aircraft? No, it was too windy for any light plane to take off. A Shackleton, perhaps, from Langebaan?

He picked up the telephone, hesitated, and then replaced it again. Caution dies hard in the civil service.

He turned up the volume on the radio and heard the call going out from Cape Town Radio's powerful transmitter.

Faintly he heard the acknowledgements from ships battering their way around the southern tip of Africa.

He picked up the coffee-pot, swilled it out in the chipped

basin which served the office as a sink, and added fresh water and coffee. He had a feeling it was going to be a long night. There was a dark and windy twilight on the sea.

*   *   *

It was six before Harry could persuade Thelma to come home. She stumbled as he helped her across the street and he realised that she was very drunk. He walked around and opened the door for her. She collapsed weakly on the seat, staring without expression through the windscreen.

He got in, slamming the door, and they drove up the empty street. He realised suddenly that he was very hungry. He stopped at a small café up the street and switched off the engine.

'I'm going to get a sandwich,' he said. 'You want one?'

'No,' she said. 'No. I can't eat. I can't think of eating.'

'You should have something,' said Harry.

'Nothing. I can't eat.'

He went into the small café. The fluorescent strip-lighting was a painful brightness.

The café smelled of burned fat and coffee and hot metal.

There were two boys in one corner, playing noisily with the pinball machine.

They looked curiously at him as he came in.

He went up to the counter and the proprietor wiped his hands on his trousers and said, 'Yes, please?'

He was a fat man with a long straight nose and thick curling black hair. Harry thought he was Greek.

He ordered a toasted sandwich and a glass of milk and sat with his elbows on the steel-topped counter.

The proprietor brought his order and slid it across the counter to him.

'From Johannesburg?' said the proprietor. He could see the Lincoln parked outside. The light from the café lit up the registration plates.

Harry nodded. 'Yes.' He didn't want to talk.

'Good place,' said the fat man. 'I lived there once, too much crime, though. I had a coffee-bar in Hillbrow. Two Fridays in a row they rob me, beat my cashier, take all the money. So I think, this is no good, and I come down here.'

'It's a rough city,' said Harry.

The fat man was looking at the Lincoln again. Harry finished his sandwich and drank the milk.

It was tepid and just starting to sour.

He paid his bill and walked out to the car. The wind was still blowing and it seemed to be colder.

A torn newspaper made a dry skittering on the pavement.

He drove slowly out of the town and up the narrow road to the cottage. When he was clear of the buildings he could feel the wind buffet the car.

9

The wind was stronger in the late afternoon and the foam it whipped from the crests was a dirty yellow.

The clouds were low and thick, and lightning flickered in

them. It started raining suddenly, hissing into the sea.

The wind drove it across the sea in stinging eddies. It lashed their faces and the serang had to screw his eyes tight. The rain was very cold and it ran down his face and down his neck and soon his clothes were sodden and the wind whipped right through them and he felt the goose-pimples rise on his skin.

Late in the afternoon they passed a ship. He saw it when they were on a crest.

It was a long way away, almost hidden by the waves. When the rain curtain lifted for a few seconds he saw white upperworks and a smudge of smoke. It was at least five miles away and he knew that it would never see them in this broken sea. The boy saw him looking and sat up and peered through the rain. The serang looked quickly away and hoped the boy would not see the ship.

'What's — ' said the boy. Then he jumped up and grabbed the mast and pointed. 'A ship! Geez, where's the flare. Hey, where's the flare?'

'Too far,' said Pillay. 'They never see it. Better we save it for some other ship. They'll never see it in this.'

The boy was on his knees at the locker, looking desperately for the flares.

He found one and stood up, stuffing the others back in the locker. The rain on his face looked like tears.

'How do you work this again?'

Pillay reached up and took it from him.

'You're wasting it,' he said. 'It's too far.'

'Give it to me,' shouted Faraday. 'Geez, give it to me.'

He was shouting and his mouth was twisted with anger.

Pillay bent down and put the flare back in the locker. The boy grabbed for the locker door and Pillay took his hand above the wrist and bent it back away from the door.

Faraday swung his other hand and Pillay turned away so that he took the blow with his shoulder.

'Get your hands off me, you bloody coolie,' Faraday shouted.

He was almost hysterical with anger. He tried to kick Pillay and Pillay turned the kick with his leg.

'You coolie. You stinking lousy bloody stinking coolie.'

He sat heavily on the thwart and suddenly he was crying with anger and humiliation.

Pillay sat back and did not look at the boy. There was no anger in him now, although he had felt it coming when the boy hit him.

Now he just felt sorry and ashamed and slightly apprehensive.

They rose on a swell and he looked quickly astern. He could not see the ship.

It had been too far away, in the rain and spray. The rain hissed harder and the smooth water in the lee of the boat was pocked with raindrops.

'It's gone,' he said to the boy. 'It was too far.'

The boy sat on the thwart and looked between his feet and said nothing. His hair was very wet and slicked down on his skull.

He was sitting with his arms on his thighs and his big tanned hands hung limply between his legs.

'I'm sorry,' said Pillay. The boy took no notice. To hell with him, thought Pillay. To hell with him and his rich father and his rich father's money and the whole lot of them, all of them, the tourists with their cameras and the game fishermen and the campers who argue about the price of fish.

He shut his mind to the boy and his kind very resolutely. All I have to worry about is keeping us afloat. That's all. They will come looking for us, all right. He settled down to sail the boat.

A big wet gust smacked them hard and they heeled very badly. The boy slid from the thwart and rolled across the bottom boards, his hands and feet scrabbling for a grip.

Pillay let the sheet fly and the sail flapped cracklingly free but the sheet whipped back and snagged the engine housing and before Pillay could free it the sail had filled hard and then split from head to foot.

It made a loud ripping noise and the two pieces of brown canvas wrapped themselves around the mast and the gaff.

Pillay sat very still, looking at the torn sail. Now it is finished, he thought.

Now there is nothing I can do. Anything I do now will just be temporary. The sea wants us and it is going to have us.

It has just been playing with us until now. He looked at the long oars lashed fore-and-aft. There are the oars. I can hold her head to sea with the oars. But that will be fighting and we can no longer fight. It is a waste of strength. He wanted to lie down and sleep and let the sea take them. He saw the boy looking at him.

Faraday had skinned his knee when he had fallen and the blood, diluted by the rain, had run in a pink smear down his leg.

Pillay sighed and stood up.

He struck the mast and wrapped the stays around it and lashed it fore and aft against the port gunwale.

He unlashed the long oars quickly, tugging impatiently at the wet rope. He did not cut the knots because good seamen do not cut knots.

When the oars were loose he dropped the crutches in the gunwale and shipped the oars, crossing the looms and hooking them under opposite gunwales.

The boat had fallen off into the troughs and was rolling very badly. He stepped amidships and sat down in the middle of the thwart, bracing his legs against the engine housing and keeping his thighs together.

Then he flexed his fingers and wrapped his hands around the handles. He looked up at the waves and thought, this is going to kill me if I'm not careful. The boy sat watching him.

He dropped the port oar into the water and heaved on it, turning the bow into the sea.

The boat came around slowly. When she was facing the waves he used the other oar, pulling very slowly and steadily, just enough to keep her from drifting astern or yawing.

At first it was easy and not at all tiring. But as the dark came the wind freshened and the waves became steeper. He could see them coming by the starlight and the whiteness of the foam on the crests.

They made a loud hissing noise in the darkness. The whole night seemed to be made of noise. Then the moon rose and it was better.

He was pulling in long steady strokes, pulling the looms into his stomach and leaning far forward with the blades held vertically while he watched the coming swells.

When the bow started to rise and he could hear the tearing of the water on the crest he put the blades down sharply and deep and leaned back, pulling hard until he could go no further, feeling the blades bite into the water.

The looms bent under the strain and he prayed aloud that they should not break:

'God, watch those oars. Please God, watch my good oars.'

They bent and creaked and ground against the crutch but the ash was good and well oiled and they did not break, but sprang straight when he lifted the shining, dripping blades and bent forward and sunk them and heaved back, again and again and again, until there was a dull hotness in his stomach and his shoulders ached and he could not see for sweat in his eyes. Good oars, he thought. Good oars.

He rowed on into the dark and roaring night. He had to keep looking over his shoulder to see the waves. He wished the boy would wake and watch the sea for him. His neck was stiff. The waves would build up behind him and he would feel *Friend* stagger and lift and then the crest would tear with a hissing behind him and he would dig the blades deep and lean back to get *Poor Man's Friend* over the top.

There were bad moments when it seemed as though he had not enough strength to pull them over the crest, and the boat would hesitate on the crest with the white water hissing around her before she slid down into the trough.

His mouth was dry and he wanted a drink of water more badly than he had ever wanted anything but he could not leave the oars.

His hands had split and they stung and he had a hot pain deep

86

in his chest now. One more pull, you strong old bastard, he told himself. Just one more pull. Good. Now another. Right, now one more. And a very last one. Oh one more before you give up. You cannot give up now. Just one more pull.

He started talking to himself, forcing the words out in gasps. Pull. Pull. Pull. He was back in a whaler and the coxswain was shouting the stroke. Pull you idle lot. Pull for your lives you bastards. Pull. He was stroke in *Fleur's* whaler when they beat the whole flotilla in Lourenço Marques Bay. Pull like that again. Oh but he wanted a drink. Tomorrow you can drink. Tonight you must pull. The stars and sea whirled about him in a roaring white-shot darkness.

Then he rowed without talking or thinking, just looking at the starboard blade as it entered the water, counting the strokes to himself, not noticing the waves or the wind or even the pain in his stomach.

The boy had to shake him before he turned his head. The boy was standing behind him, feet wide on the boards. The wind was blowing his light hair and in the starlight Pillay could see the peeling skin on his forehead.

'I'll take them,' said Faraday. Pillay kept pulling.

'It's fine,' he said. 'I'm okay.'

'I'll take them now,' said Faraday. He pushed Pillay's shoulder. 'You take a break. I'll take them.'

'It's all right,' said Pillay. 'I'm fine. You sleep. I'm fine.' His voice was thick with lack of sleep and the words came out slurred, as though he were drunk.

'I'm going to,' said Faraday.

He was very determined now that he had made up his mind. He put his arms around Pillay and gripped the handles.

Pillay bent and slipped under the oars and Faraday sat down. They had not missed a stroke.

Pillay ducked under the oars again and stepped over the thwart and went aft. He lay down on the boards and pulled the torn sail over him and was instantly asleep.

His head rested on the turn of the bilge and rolled slightly with the movement of the boat.

The wind slackened towards morning and rowing was easier. The grey clouds were very high and tattered in the cold morning light and the moon was still up.

It was very cold. The waves were smaller and only occasionally breaking. Faraday slid the oars across the boat, port loom under starboard gunwale and starboard loom under port gunwale and sucked in deep breaths. The air was very cold.

He could feel it in his throat. He unlashed the water-can and took a small drink, holding the water in his mouth for a long time before swallowing it.

The ache went from his arms and thighs, leaving them stiff. We held her, he thought. We held her into the sea all night. He felt proud of the achievement. It was something.

He looked at the sleeping Malay and his own tiredness caught him by surprise and washed over him so that he swayed on the thwart.

He shook his head and scooped sea-water in his hands and washed his face.

He sat shivering in the morning breeze and looked at the serang sleeping with his dark brown face on the boards. There was a white stubble on his cheeks and jaws. Why, thought the boy, he is an old man.

His anger had all gone now and he was ashamed of the way he had behaved. For two days the serang had held the boat by himself. I sulked, he thought. I sulked like a naughty child. Now perhaps it's too late. He tried to work out how long they had been adrift but his mind refused to accept the problem. It just skimmed around and around on the surface of his mind and his mind veered away and he could not remember. He thought it was two days. Or three. He wondered if they were searching for them.

He felt sorry for his father. Then he remembered his mother and felt even more sorry for his father. He did not think he was going to die in this boat. It was still an adventure. An uncomfortable one, but an adventure.

He looked at the serang and wondered whether he was Coloured or Malay.

He has the wide face and the nose of a Malay, he thought. Pillay opened his eyes and sat up. The sail crackled as he pushed it aside and the dew ran off and trickled across the boards.

Pillay leaned over the side and washed his face. He took a mouthful of sea-water and swished it around his mouth and spat it out.

'You shouldn't have let me sleep all night,' he said. There was a wide yellow strip in the east now and the clouds were lying in thin black streaks above it.

'That's all right,' said Faraday. He went aft and pulled the sail over him. The underside of the sail was quite warm.

He lay on the edge of sleep and watched Pillay making the fire.

He slept and when he awoke the sun was well up and it

was warmer. He pushed aside the sail and crawled to the fire.

Pillay was cooking the last piece of the katonkel. There was very little left.

10

The young men in their brown flying suits walked across the oil-streaked concrete to the planes. The stubby Harvards were in line abreast.

They were silver-grey with the numerals in black on the sides of their fuselages. Their noses and the tips of their wings were painted with bright orange fluorescent paint. It was supposed to reduce the chances of them flying into each other.

They walked to their planes and slung their parachute packs on to the tailplanes and shrugged into them. The wind was already gusty and it whistled in the radio aerials and sighed around the wings. Far across the field they could see the windsock.

They climbed into the cockpits and slammed the canopies and there was the coughing metallic clatter of six big engines starting from cold. Smoke squirted from the exhausts and the engines spat and choked. The propellers were whirling yellow-tipped discs. The engine roar bounced back from the walls of the hangars.

A mechanic came to the door of the nearest hangar and watched the leading Harvard wiggle its flaps and rudder and taxi slowly up the ramp to the grass.

The other five followed in line, bumping over the joins in the concrete like tired ducks. The mechanic went back inside the hangar. He had seen it before.

The Harvards bumped slowly across the field and on to the east-west runway. A flock of big hadedah birds flapped away with protesting croaks. The birds were always feeding on the airfield. They ate the locusts which lived in the coarse grass. Today a flock of starlings were feeding with them, and three or four white egrets.

The egrets were afraid of the planes and spiralled up into the windy sky.

The lead pilot looked at the birds sourly. They should be shot.

One day a plane was going to collect one, in the prop or through the canopy. One of the Viscounts, probably, and what a mess that would be.

He taxied past the tower and waved absently. Then they were up at the end of the runway and turning into the wind.

He had a hangover and a headache behind the eyes and the last thing he felt like was a long search. He had been on searches before. No matter how hard they looked they never found anything. He switched on his radio.

'Okay?' he asked. Voices crackled back at him. He opened the throttle wide, holding the plane on its brakes.

The big engine bellowed and the grass beside the concrete lay flat.

He held it open for several seconds while his head ached and the airframe throbbed and quivered and then he released the brakes, easing the throttle, and the Harvards rolled down the concrete, in line, bouncing a little as they gained speed, and then lifted, swaying, into the wind, climbing over the red roofs of the town, the bright turquoise swimming bath, the wind-patterned beach with its slow-creaming surf, tucking up their wheels and turning south. They climbed slowly to three thousand feet and flew at one hundred and sixty knots. Far below six shadows chased them across the wrinkled dark green sea.

From that height the sea looked very calm. The wave crests were slow-moving crescents. In the shallows the pilots could see the dark shadows of reefs.

They had flown over the sea a hundred times and it no longer interested them.

They followed the coastline for thirty minutes and then turned seawards.

The wind had increased and the planes rocked in sharp gusts. It grew warm in the cockpits and the pilots sweated in their flying suits, strapped into their seats, criss-crossed with parachute harness. The radio was a dry crackle.

– keep your eyes open

– ja

– be hard to find in that mess down there

– the day we find anything I'll chop

– that's enough of the natter, keep your eyes open

– ja, boss.

And droning on into the hot windy morning.

They looked very carefully, diving to look at a log, a distant ship; knowing they would find nothing, and yet hoping all the time that they would. The sea unrolled behind them: blue foam-flecked, empty, and stretched before them to the southern end of the world.

The lead pilot opened his canopy and listened to the slipstream buffeting the aircraft. His head still ached and the search depressed him.

All the searches he had ever been on depressed him. Once, just once, he thought, I'd like to find a boat, dive over it, circle, see the men wave, knowing they were saved.

I'd like to fly home imagining their faces and walk into the mess and have a beer and think of how they must have felt when they saw me. But it never happens that way.

We just burn up the taxpayer's money and never find anything. But it's good training. He was a permanent force instructor and the other five pilots were in the Citizen Force. It's good training and the boys like it. Me, I don't like it.

I don't like to think of some poor wog adrift down there, waiting and waiting and slowly giving up.

He looked down at the sea and banked slowly to starboard.

– okay, boys. Home.

– Good-oh.

Going home they had the wind up their tails and they made good time.

They landed in close formation and taxied back to the hangar and unstrapped their parachutes and walked stiffly to the mess, parachutes dangling down their backs.

– not a bloody thing

– wild goose chase

– never is a thing

The lead pilot walked across the concrete to his office and

took off his flying suit and hung it up in a steel cupboard against the wall facing the airfield.

He put his parachute on a shelf near the door.

He was putting on his tie when the squadron's commanding officer came in.

The commanding officer was a Citizen Force captain who was a lawyer in private life.

He had a very good war record in the Western Desert and Korea and he had joined the Citizen Force because he liked flying.

He did not do much flying now but he still liked being around aircraft. He was a small neat man with bright sharp eyes.

He came into the office with a tall tanned man. The pilot looked at the stranger's eyes and the set of his mouth and knew who he was without being told. He had seen that look before. Too often before.

'This is Mr Koenig,' said the Citizen Force captain. 'Lieutenant Botha.'

They shook hands.

'Mr Koenig's boy is in the boat,' said the captain.

'I'm sorry,' said Botha.

'Nothing?' said the captain. 'No luck?' He felt he should still keep it light.

'No sir,' said Botha. 'Nothing at all. I'm very sorry', he said, looking at Koenig.

'Well,' said Koenig. He looked out at the Harvards lined up on the strip.

'Well, thank you very much indeed, all of you. Will you thank the other men for me?'

He turned and walked out of the office and into the sunlight and the wind.

Botha watched them walk across the strip to Koenig's car. Then he went across to the mess and bought a beer. He sat in a corner and drank it slowly, looking out at the airfield. He could see the green glass control tower and the windsock.

He ordered another beer and when it came he walked across and joined the others at the bar.

The captain came into the mess and stood at the door looking for the lieutenant. Botha stood up and the captain walked over to him.

'Beer, sir?' asked Botha.

The barman opened a beer and slopped a little into a glass and handed the glass and the bottle to the captain.

'Thanks,' said the captain. 'Cheers.'

'Cheers.'

'I'm going to ask Cape Town for a Shackleton,' said the captain. 'I think they're far out.'

'If they're still afloat,' said Botha.

'Yes. But those little boats are tough. And I hear this old man's a good skipper. I've been on the blower to Bloubaai and the harbour master tells me he's the best man on the coast.'

'They've had a tug out,' said Botha.

'Yes. And one of the frigates – *Louw Wepenaar*, I think – has been diverted to search. She's on her way back from Marion Island.'

'A hell of a lot of people and money,' said Botha.

'You mean for a coolie?'

'I guess that's what I mean.'

'We've done it before,' said the captain.

He sounded angry.

'You know we've done it before. It doesn't make any difference that there's Koenig's kid in the boat. We've mounted bigger searches than this before, just for some bloody line-boat that's overdue with a crowd of drunken Coloureds.'

'I know,' said Botha. 'But somehow that sort of story never gets into the overseas newspapers. This one will.'

'You're getting cynical,' said the captain.

'I guess so,' said the lieutenant.

'If you consider it a waste of time, just look at it as good training,' said the captain.

'No sir,' said Botha. 'I don't consider it a waste of time at all. It's just that we never find them.'

'You're just feeling down today,' said the captain. 'On the pots last night?'

'A little, sir,' said Botha.

'Have another one,' said the captain.

The barman put two more beers on the counter. They were very cold and small peaks of foam showed at the necks of the bottles.

'It's good public relations,' said the captain.

'I know, sir,' said Botha.

'The public expects us to go out. That's what we're here for, they think.'

'Yes sir. I just wish we found somebody sometime.'

'Oh well,' said the captain. 'Don't let it get you down.'

'No sir. I won't do that.'

'How's the wife?' asked the captain. 'How's Toy?' He prided himself on taking an interest in the private lives of his men.

'Oh, fine,' said Botha. 'She's fine.'

'That's good,' said the captain. He finished his beer and went out. The other young men stopped playing liar-dice on the bar counter and one of them opened the door for him. They all said good night to him as he went out. He was a very popular officer.

Through the window they could see him walking very smartly and erect to his car.

Botha ordered another beer and stood at the window and looked at the darkening airfield and the flapping windsock. He was thinking of the men in the boat. He drank the beer in big gulps and went back to the bar and bought another.

His hangover was quite gone now. He walked over to the men playing liar-dice and accepted another beer. The barman took his glass away and gave him one of the big tankards the mess used for special occasions. It held a quart of beer and it had a glass bottom so that when he tilted it to his mouth he could see the bar through it with the men all twisted and distorted through the beer and the thick glass. He stood there watching the men through the glass and wished the captain had not mentioned his wife. Now he was determined to enjoy himself that evening. He stood there with the big pewter tankard held to his face like a telescope and watched the men and the field beyond the windows and wished the captain had never mentioned his wife. She had told him that morning that she was in love with another man. He was only twenty-three and it hurt like hell. Damn it, he thought. It would really have been kinder on this day if we had found something, for all of us.

11

In the morning the sea was calm and very blue under the clear sky.

They were drifting very slowly now. It became hot as the sun rose higher and the serang made a tent of the small sail and they sat under it.

Towards noon they saw birds diving ahead of them. They were big black and white birds and they wheeled flashing in the sunlight, dropping into the water like bombs.

'Malgas,' said the serang. He sat watching the diving birds.

'After sardine, I guess.'

They were still a mile away. When they drifted closer they could hear their harsh crying across the water. Then they could see the shoal, like a brown stain on the blue sea. Fish kept breaking the water in small wild flurries and the birds were falling into the sea. Some of the big birds floated, gorged, on the edge of the shoal. There are probably big fish under the shoal, thought the serang. Katonkel or bonito. Maybe tunny. He took his bloodline from the locker and smoothed the tattered feathers of the lure.

They drifted into the shoal and the floating birds flapped clumsily away, screaming.

The serang dropped the lure over the stern and it went straight down into the clear blue water. They were not drifting fast enough for it to stream astern or have any movement which would attract a fish.

The black line went vertically into the water and the red feathers dangled uselessly beneath the boat. If there was just a little wind, thought the serang. He rested his chin on the gunwale and looked into the water.

Far below he could see the red spot of the lure. Four big fish swam steadily beneath the boat and vanished into the blue distance. They were dark blue and had smooth round heads. He thought they were yellowtail.

In the middle of the shoal the water was dotted with dead and dying sardines, leftovers of the birds' feeding. The serang and Faraday scooped up as many as they could and laid them carefully on the thwart. They lay in a shimmering row in the bright sunlight. When there were no more within reach they cleaned the ones they had, slicing them up the small ridged bellies and scooping out the small guts, and eating them raw. They were nearly out of the shoal now.

The birds had stopped diving and were sitting on the water.

The shark came up astern as they were eating the last of the fish.

He was a very big hammerhead, high-shouldered and shovel-headed, and he swam with his dorsal fin and the upper lobe of his tail high out of the water.

He swam with a slight roll, moving his wide flat head from side to side. His back was a deep gun-metal grey with a shading of bronze, and his belly was a glistening white. He swam past the *Friend* and turned slowly. They could see his gills fluttering in the clear water.

'Oh, you big deformity,' said Pillay softly. Like many fishermen, he believed that hammerheads were deformed sharks.

'Oh, you big deformity.' The boy sat up and said, 'What's that?'

'Hammerhead,' said the serang. 'Big one.'

'Let's see,' said Faraday. He scrambled across the boat and knelt in the stern sheets.

The shark shied away, stirring the water with its high tail. Then it turned and came slowly back. They could see the flat cold eyes at the tips of the hammer.

Faraday felt suddenly cold.

'What's it waiting for?'

Pillay shrugged.

'They often hang 'round fishing boats. Waiting for us to get fish, I guess.

'Well, he's unlucky today.'

He looked at the big fish lying so quietly in the water.

'You can — off, *haai*,' he said. 'We got no fish today.'

Then he remembered the bloodline. I hope he doesn't see that lure. He put his hand on the bloodline and began to take it in very slowly.

The shark stirred and swam closer and he stopped hauling in the line. The shark put its head down and slid into the blue.

Oh, now it comes, thought the serang. I should have left the line alone. All these years and I make mistakes. He felt the first questing nudge on the lure and then the line started running out between his fingers.

He stepped back and made sure that the line could run free. It ran out steadily and he let it go without any pressure.

Run, you deformity. Run and swallow that lure deep so that I can hook you in the guts. Do that, or spit it out. I want you to spit it out, but if you won't I want to hook you deep so that you die easily.

But the line kept running out between his fingers and over the gunwale and when the fish had taken fifty feet he knew it was not going to spit the lure out.

He checked the line across the palm of his hand and swung his arm back, hard, feeling the hook drive into something solid. Then the line was whipping painfully through his hands and into the water with a dry zit-zit-zit across the gunwale.

'My glove,' he said to the boy.

'My glove, quick.'

Faraday opened the locker and took out the old motor gauntlet and Pillay transferred the line to his left hand while he slipped the gauntlet on to his right.

The gauntlet was old and worn, scarred by many lines.

He twisted the line around his arm and let it run across his palm, through his clenched fingers.

He was holding as hard as he could, to break the fish while he was still fresh.

He knew he could not fight a big fish for long.

The shark was swimming faster now and the line was rising through the water.

Pillay could feel the gauntlet growing warm with the friction. He slacked off the tension a little and the shark swam faster.

He tightened up a little again but the shark kept going. It was really going now.

The line hissed into the water and tore the surface in a thin line of foam.

Man, he's really going, thought Pillay.

He felt the old fisherman's excitement coming up in him. Man, he's going like a train. Like an express train. He thought of the hammerhead as a big flat-headed high-shouldered train boring through the dark tunnel of the sea.

The pull on the line was really solid. The shark had his head down and was boring deep.

The first wild panic, when he felt the hook, was gone now and he was settling down to fight. Looking down at the line hissing into the dark blue water Pillay could imagine the gleam of the wire leader curving back across the high back and the impatient sideways jerk of the head, like a bit-shy horse, as the hammerhead tried to throw the hook.

But you won't throw this one, you big deformity. This one is in deep. I felt it go in. I've hooked you good.

Now that he had the shark on he was glad and excited. He was too good a fisherman not to be excited by the feel of a big fish, even if it was only a shark.

But in any case hammerheads fought. They were not like the lazy yellow-bellies who allowed themselves to be dragged in with hardly a struggle.

No, this was a fighting shark. This was a shark that ran like an express train.

The shark began a wide circle and Pillay snubbed the line and held on but the shark was still fresh and he had to give a little. He gave it reluctantly, inch by inch, but the shark kept going. But the first long rush had stopped. I'm glad of that. The first run is the worst. If you don't get broken on the first run you've usually got them, 'less you do something silly. Sometimes they come up and thresh around on top, shaking their head. This one's not going to do that yet. He's a deep fighter. Well, that's okay with me. Let him fight deep and kill himself that way. I got plenty of line and I'm not tired yet.

The sun was very hot in the faded sky and it lanced down into the water so that he could see the dustmotes dancing for a long way down.

The line stopped hissing in the water and the foam drifted away and Pillay could see the tight black thread of the line disappearing through the sunlight into the dark blue. He's a long way down, he thought. The line was still running out but more slowly now.

There was a twanging on the taut line now. The shark was swinging his body and thumping the line with his tail. The line kept rising up through the blue clear water.

Then the shark came up a hundred yards away. It came up with a loud tearing sound and rolled, shaking its head and slamming the water with its tail. Then it went down again, deep and very fast.

Now, thought Pillay. Now I must kill it very quickly. He sat in the stern sheets and took the line in both hands, wrapping it around his forearms, and held. My Lord, he thought, but this deformity is strong.

The line hummed across the gunwale and dried blood flaked from it and fell on the planks.

He felt the boat move and he gave the shark some more line. The fish made a big circle around the boat and he stood up to stop the line fouling around the propeller.

The black line made an arc of thin white foam in the water.

I must kill him quickly, thought Pillay. He hit the shark again, nearly losing his balance.

The shark was solid at the end of the line and when Pillay dropped his arm forward and then jerked it back it was as though he had hit a rock.

The shark moved away very quickly, the line zit-zit-zit across the grooved gunwale and hissing in the water and cutting into the gauntlet. I've hurt him, thought Pillay.

Now he has really felt the hook.

He put one foot on the stern sheets and rested his right arm on his thigh.

His arm was tired now and his biceps were aching from keeping the pressure up.

As he stood there his leg began jumping with a nervous twitch in the calf muscles. He could not stop it jumping on the stern sheets.

He leaned hard on his leg but the twitching and the jumping remained.

He wished that the shark would break loose so that he could rest.

Then he remembered that the shark would have a big liver, it being such a big shark, for shark's livers are all disproportionate to the size of their bodies; and the price for shark livers was sixpence a pound. Shark liver oil is richer than cod liver oil.

So he stopped wishing that the shark could break away and set about killing it as quickly as possible.

The thought of the shark's liver had brought out all the fisherman in him. But he was still very tired and his leg was still jumping.

Still, that was nothing to worry about. He had seen it happen before when men had a big fish on. But it had never happened to him before and he did not like it. The boy was looking at his leg.

'What's wrong with your leg?' he asked. Pillay tried to smile but the tension in his face pulled his mouth crooked.

'Nothing,' he said. 'Jus' twitches. Nothing.'

The boy sat down and watched the taut line cutting the water.

'It's a big one,' he said. He was not so angry any more. The sun had baked the anger out of him. He just wanted to get home and have a decent meal and sleep in a decent bed with clean hard white sheets. He closed his eyes against the glare from the sea and wished they were home.

There was a new motion on the end of the line. Pillay could feel a twisting, irregular jerk. The shark was rolling. He felt sudden elation. That meant it was tired. He thought of the trace he had the lure on. It was four feet of twisted wire, swivelled at the lure and where it was looped on to the blood-line.

It would not kink and snap. But if the shark rolled enough the wire would twist around his body and perhaps the line would chafe against his skin, or perhaps he would get the line between his teeth as he threshed.

He put both legs on the floor-boards and leaned hard on the line, swaying his body and swinging his arm. Easy, easy. Don't break it now.

The irregular movement stopped and he knew the shark was swimming straight again.

He kept on the pressure, feeding the line out very reluctantly, holding it as hard as he could, snubbing it with his heavy gauntlet.

The line had cut new criss-cross furrows in the leather.

The shark swam faster. Pillay had to give more line. He felt as though the line were being pulled out of him, as though it was his intestines that were being dragged into the sea.

He looked quickly over his shoulder at the pile of red-black line on the boards. It was very small. The coils were lifting, still stiff with the dried blood, and snaking across the boards, between his legs, through the gauntlet and over the side. He could see the boards through the remainder of the pile.

There were only a few turns left on the boards when the shark stopped its run. Now, thought Pillay.

He started recovering the line with long strong pulls and the pile on the boards grew. Sometimes the shark would start a run again and the wet line would slip through Pillay's fingers, but he would always stop it after a yard or two and keep taking it in.

The shark was coming up now, making another wide circle of the boat.

The line came slowly up through the water and the pile on the boards grew thicker, shining black and wet, showing white patches where tension had jumped the blood off.

Pillay's arms were aching badly and his leg was still twitching, but not so badly now that he was standing square.

He was getting the line in faster now. Water from the line soaked the gauntlet and ran down his arms and splashed on his trousers.

The shark came up fifty feet away and made a splashing on the surface.

They could see its high tail and the dorsal fin, and then the wide pelvic fins, white underneath, as it rolled.

'Now,' said the serang. His voice was hoarse and it came out like a gasp. 'Now. Not long now.'

The shark steadied and swam in a wide circle around the boat and Pillay kept swinging it nearer, taking in the line without a pause, with long swings of his arms.

Now he no longer tried to coil the recovered line so that it could run out freely if the shark made another break.

He knew he must end it now or let the shark go because he could not go on much longer.

But the shark kept coming and the circle around the boat grew tighter and tighter and then the shark was alongside, white belly up, beside the boat.

It was six feet long and the hammer was two feet across. The mouth was a wide crescent on the underside of the hammer.

Pillay picked up his kierie and leaned over the gunwale, sliding his hand down the leader until it was a foot from the shark's head. With a sudden heave he lifted the head half out of the water and turned it over, hitting it hard just where the flatness of the hammer swelled out into the neck.

The shark stirred restlessly and the tail slapped against the side of the boat and then it was still. A thread of blood trickled from the gills and clouded in the clear water.

Pillay looped the line around the thwart and drew his knife and severed the shark's back-bone. The knife was very sharp and the taut grey skin opened gapingly and showed the pale-pink flesh.

When he had finished he sat down and took a long drink of

water and waited for the trembling in his legs to go.

The boy leaned over the gunwale and looked at the dead shark.

It stirred gently in the low swell and the eyes at the ends of the hammer were flat and dull.

The teeth showed along the rim of the mouth.

They were big and white, shaped like irregular triangles, all slanting one way.

The torn red feather of the lure fluttered in one corner of the mouth. There was not much left of the feather.

The boy's mind registered that they would not be able to use the lure again, with so little of the feathers left.

Now that the excitement was over and he could feel his sunburn again, the slight nausea that had never left him rose up in his throat, sour and wet, and he leaned over the gunwale and vomited into the water.

Pillay cut a long slab of meat from the shark and sliced off the leathery grey skin. The flesh was pinkish-white and looked good.

'Can you eat shark?' asked Faraday.

'Right now, I can eat anything,' said Pillay.

'Me too. But can you eat it?'

'Yes. It taste okay, too.'

Faraday watched him cut it into thin fillets and cook it. It did not look bad. He just didn't like the idea of eating shark. That was silly. It was just a fish. Still, he did not like the idea.

Then he remembered shark-fin soup and thought it would probably be all right. And he was more hungry than he had ever been in his life. If they made soup of shark's fins and sold it in the best restaurants and made you pay through the nose for it the flesh could not be harmful. But perhaps they processed the fins from which they made the soup. He did not know. But he knew that he was painfully hungry and he was going to eat shark meat today. When it came it was not unpleasant. It was white and flaky and tasteless but not unpleasant. Salt would have given it more flavour. He looked at the shark lashed alongside and thought that at least they would have food for tomorrow. The serang passed him another slice of flesh. It was burned on one side.

'I'm full,' he said. 'I've had enough.'

He had eaten a lot and his hunger was blunted.

'We must eat all we can today,' said Pillay. 'We can't keep this. Shark won't keep. It goes bad very quick and then it is too bitter to eat.'

Faraday took the slice and laid it on the thwart.

'It'll keep for today, won't it? I'll eat it tonight.'

When they had finished the serang opened the shark's belly and lifted the liver into the boat. It was two feet long and a yellowish grey and weighed about twenty pounds.

He laid it on the boards and it quivered slightly, like jelly. There were the faint blue threads of veins in the yellow.

Pillay cut another chunk of meat from the shark and then cut the lure out of the crescent mouth and let the shark sink. It went down through the clear water in big spiralling loops and dives, belly up.

They watched it gliding down into the deep green and they could see the white glimmer of the belly for a long way down.

The clouds drifted northwards and it was very hot in the boat. There was a low swell and the water was very deep blue with shades of purple. The sun glanced off the water and hurt their eyes so they could hardly look at the sea.

Faraday was sick with the exhausted sickness which comes from too much salt water and sun and boat-motion.

He had a headache all the time now and his face stung where the skin had peeled.

His skin was stretched tight across his face and it was uncomfortable to speak. His lips had cracked and healed and cracked again and there was always the taste of blood in his mouth.

His cracked lips felt swollen. They felt like two sausages stitched to his mouth.

He sat and watched the serang searching in the locker. Pillay stood up and he had a pack of soiled cards in his hand. He came and sat down beside Faraday.

'You play?' he asked. He thumbed the cards.

'Rummy,' said Faraday. Pillay nodded.

'We play then.' He shuffled and dealt the cards out on the boards, sitting cross-legged.

'What are we playing for?' asked Faraday. It hurt him to speak and he felt his lips open again.

'Nothing. Anything. You got money?'

Faraday felt in his pocket. He had three shillings in small change. He divided it equally and they played. When they had finished he owed the serang five shillings, after Pillay had paid back his original stake.

They kept score by notching the thwart. Then it was too hot to play cards any more and they lay back with their heads under the scrap of canvas. They could feel the sun through the canvas. The boy lay and thought about Pillay.

'What's a serang?' he asked. He spoke carefully, without moving his lips.

'A sort of boss-boy. You know on the harbours, stevedores, that work in the ships?'

'Yes. Is a serang a stevedore?'

'Uhuh. He's a sort of boss-boy of a gang of them. And anyway, they're not all stevedores. Really the stevedore is the big shot. The others is just dockers.'

'Oh,'

He lay and thought about it.

'Did you save up and buy this boat?'

'Yes. It took a long time.'

'Oh,' said the boy.

He had never had to save for anything. Yes, he had. He remembered. When he had first wanted a bicycle his father had said he would have to save his pocket money towards it. He had started saving but then it was his birthday and the bicycle was standing at the foot of his bed when he awoke that morning and so he took the money he had saved and spent it on something else, he could not remember what.

'He is a good boat,' said Pillay.

'I thought boats were always called she.'

'Not *Poor Man's Friend*. He's a cock boat.'

Then it was too hot to talk any more and when they stopped talking he felt the sun come suddenly lower and it was as though it were hanging just above his head. All the skin on his face and head tightened. He could feel the tension on his scalp and his lips felt like wood now. His whole body felt encased. His eyes kept watering and his vision seemed to be narrowing in from the sides, as though his eyes were being shuttered horizontally, like a bird's. He lay on the boards with his head as far in the shadow as he could get it and tried hard to think of home.

He tried to imagine his father and mother when he finally returned but he could not remember their faces. He tried hard to imagine them but the image was blurred. He groaned aloud and the serang sat up quickly, pushing the sail back so that the sun stabbed his face.

'You all right? You all right, Boss?' There was concern in his face. Faraday rolled his head away.

'Yes. I'm all right. Yes. Oh Jeez, that sun burns.' Pillay lay down and pulled the sail back over them. The boat rocked gently and the sea slapped the hull, gently. The sky was a white flame.

If they're going to pray, thought Pillay, they'd better not leave it too long now. No sense wastin' it.

'You like some water?' he asked Faraday.

'Uhuh. No. I'll be fine.'

12

On the fifth morning the westerly blew again. It started very early in the morning, slapping across the sea with the first pale light. When the sun was still a thin red peeling it was knocking the tops off the waves.

The morning was grey and cold and wet with the spray

from the waves and now all sense of adventure, all the stimu-
lant of excitement, had gone away and only the dull weariness
remained.

Faraday lay curled on the hard boards like a tired dog, with
his arms wrapped across his shoulders. His face hurt where the
skin had peeled. There were small sunburn-scabs on his
cheekbones, where the skin was pulled tight, and on his chin.
He wished he had some olive oil for his face. They had always
used olive oil back home. It was the best sunburn lotion there
was. He lay curled up on his side and looked at the water
slopping in the bilge and noticed that a thin green slime was
growing on the boards.

Pillay crouched in front of the brazier, puffing on the small
flames which licked reluctantly at the damp splinters. He
sensed Farrie looking at him and cocked his head.

'Pretty soon we tear this whole old boat apart,' he said.
He was trying very hard to be cheerful.

'Your old man buy me a new boat if I tear this one up
cooking for his son?'

'Perhaps,' said Farrie. His lips hurt when he spoke. 'Just
maybe.'

There were two small strips of cooked shark left and
Pillay heated them over the small fire. When they were
warmed he brought them across and sat cross-legged on the
boards beside the boy.

'Breakfast, Boss. Crisp bacon followed by fried eggs an'
toast for the favourite guests. Nothing but the best in this
hotel.'

The meat was blackened with smoke and tasted of
ammonia.

'Force it down,' said Pillay. 'It won't kill you. *Wat nie dood maak, maak vet*, remember.'

They finished the fish and drank some water and that was their breakfast.

Pillay sat with his legs stretched across the boat. He felt quite suddenly very tired and he felt his age for the first time. For him the adventure had stopped long ago. He had had enough adventures. Adventures were for young men and he had learned with a sudden quick painful insight that he was no longer a young man. If he ever got out of this he would remember that he was no longer young. When he caught sight of his face in the mirror over the bar he would wink at himself and he would remember it and go home.

But he would miss it. He would miss having adventures. He looked at the grey and broken sea and thought of the adventures he had enjoyed.

Without money I have still had a good life, he thought. I never thought that was possible, but I have. And exciting, although many of the things did not seem exciting at the time, only wearisome or painful or frightening. The very best time with all adventures was when they were over. He laughed at that. The very best time, yes, without much doubt the best time of any adventure was when you were telling people about it in the bar afterwards.

He remembered the night three of them had been night fishing for kob in False Bay and their old boat had quietly opened a seam and sunk under them and they had been left swimming, three of them in the cold dark night sea, a mile offshore, laughing at first, for they were all young and that night quite surprisingly sober and all good swimmers; and

114

then slowly crawling shorewards, trailing shining tails of luminous water, because the phosphorus was thick that night, until the strong spring tide turned and sucked them to sea again and separated them so that Pillay was left alone in the dark water with the high loom of the land a long way off and the water which had been warm now cold and the bright lights looping the sea-front seeming to recede from him as he swam.

He swam most of the night and when morning came and he could see the first trams clanking along the beach road he had to give up and float because he was making no progress at all and the lights, pale now in the grey dawn, were just as far as they had ever been and he was now prepared to die and too tired to worry about it.

Then just before the proper dawn the tide began pushing him again and a school of porpoises found him and began blowing and squeaking inquisitively around him. The water foamed silver when they surfaced and when they dived he could see the glow around their bodies as they dived beneath him.

They made him feel better and he started swimming again and he tried to speak to them as he swam but most of the words stayed in his head but he believed he was carrying on a most intelligent conversation with them and they stayed with him right until he hit the first low breakers.

When he came ashore he sat on the wet sand with his hands clutching his shaking legs and he looked across the bay, all silver now in the early sunlight, and he thought, did I really do that?

His legs ached when he stood up and it was painful to walk

but he staggered through the thick sand and up to the road along the tar beach road to the police station, and he told them his friends were still in the bay. They did not believe him at first, when he told them where he had swum from. A constable walked around the charge office counter and smelled his breath and then they saw his wet clothes and how exhausted he was and they telephoned the harbour for a launch to search for his friends and gave him coffee and then called the district surgeon and put him to sleep in one of the empty cells.

He slept for eleven hours and when he awoke the first thing he remembered was the porpoises. He remembered them now. He had a belief about porpoises. He believed they were the souls of good men who had loved the sea when they were alive. He believed that porpoises were the freest and best things on earth and if there was anything he wished to be except a man it was a porpoise. But for the present he was happy to be a man. He did not think men were as happy as porpoises, but there were compensations for being a man. There were, he had found, compensations in most things. He still told the story of his swim to anybody who would listen and it was usually worth a drink. He drank most nights, if he had made a catch, in a small hotel near the harbour. But he was not a heavy drinker. He would sit over three glasses of wine all night. The bar was small and the counter was topped with dented zinc.

The bar smelled of cheap wine and fish and chips and wet clothing and other less acceptable odours (there was a dirty public lavatory just outside) and on the hot nights the double swing doors were jammed open and the patrons could see the harbour if they looked in the mirror and hear the steady mutter of the sea against the wall. The barman was a very keen boxing fan and he pasted the pictures of his heroes all around the mirror. When he was keen on Joe Louis he had peeled off every other picture and made a solid frieze of Joe Louis pictures right around the mirror. That was before the war. Since then he had switched his affections many times and very few Joe Louis pictures remained uncovered. The barman was a frustrated boxer and whenever he had to eject a drunk he would square up to him like he was in the ring and tap him alongside the head, bop bop, and grin at the customers to show them how confident he was and what a boy the ring had lost. It was just his luck that he never picked on anyone who was big enough or sober enough to belt him. Most of the regulars whom he bored with his boxing talk came along every night because they reckoned that one day somebody would up and clock him a good one, which was something they couldn't do themselves if they wanted to go on using the bar, because the owner was a big fat-gutted Jewish-Afrikaner, a very rare mixture, and he wouldn't tolerate patrons who belted his barman because in every brawl of that sort a great many glasses get broken and that sort of thing cuts into the profits and the owner was a man who kept a very close eye on the profits.

Pillay had a certain standing in the bar because he had his own boat. If he had a bad day he could always get something on the book. The boxer-loving barman often indulged in horseplay with the other regulars but he left Pillay alone.

Their burned faces stung in the cold wind. The boy began shivering, his feet rat-tatting on the boards. It was a deep hard shuddering which came from deep inside him.

Pillay looked at him with concern. He felt a lot for the boy now. Faraday lay there and looked at him and his eyes were like a frightened dog's. Pillay pulled off his jersey and tossed it across the boat. Faraday pulled it over his head and put his arms into the sleeves. It was too big for him and it hung on him like a sack, but it was knitted of thick oiled wool and it kept the wind out.

'Thank you,' he said. He sat up and pulled his knees up under his chin.

'Aren't you cold?'

'Not very,' said Pillay. 'I've got my fat to keep me warm.' He patted his stomach. It was not a big stomach, really. The boy looked doubtful.

'Are you sure?'

'Sure.'

'I'm sorry,' said Faraday. 'About that – that other time.'

'That's okay,' said Pillay. He wished the boy wouldn't talk about it. 'That's okay. You just forget about all that.'

'I didn't want to be rude,' said the boy. 'You know that?'

'Sure, sure. I know how it is. Don't you worry about that.'

'It's just the way things are,' said Faraday. 'You know that?'

'I know that,' said Pillay. I surely know that, he thought. If there's one thing I know, it's that.

'I didn't mean it the way it sounded,' said Faraday. 'Not like you were dirty, or not good enough, or anything like that.'

'You just said it wrong,' said Pillay. He felt suddenly bitter and wished he could shut up. Shut up, you coolie, he told himself. The boy was looking at him now, worried.

'What you must learn is to do it right,' he said, hating

himself for picking on a boy and yet unable to stop himself. 'You must learn to insult people nicely. You must insult people so's it's a humane act. You must be rude in a civilised way. So's it doesn't hurt, so's you don't feel bad about it.'

'I didn't mean it that way,' said Faraday.

'I know. I'm sorry.'

'When we get ashore I'll tell them, tell them how it was.'

'That won't do no good. People won't be told nothing they don't want to know. You go back, tell people you wore a coolie's jersey, you know what they'll say? They'll say, whoo, man, you better wash yourself with Dettol quick, take a good long bath in it, sonny.'

'I'll tell them,' said the boy. 'It won't be like that when I tell them.'

'You'll see,' said Pillay.

'I don't believe it,' said the boy: and then he saw his mother's face and he knew it was true.

The wind blew away the clouds and it grew hotter. They lay under the sail and panted like stranded fish. Faraday tried to sleep. He tried counting sheep but that had never worked for him and he gave up after a few minutes. His skin prickled with dried sweat and salt and his eyes felt as if there was grit under the lids. Even the eyeballs felt tender.

He wanted a drink of water but he knew there was not much left. I'll wait an hour, he decided. That's – his head throbbed with the simple sum – three thousand six hundred seconds. One hour. Three thousand seconds. He started counting. He lost count after a few hundred and started again. The figures tumbled over themselves in his head. He couldn't do it. He couldn't even count any more. He turned his head away quickly so the serang wouldn't see the tears of frustration trickling down his cheeks. He swore at himself, silently. Stop it, oh stop it, stop crying you bloody sissy and pull yourself together.

He sat up, keeping his face turned away from the old man, and looked at the moving sea and the hard bright sky, empty from horizon to horizon, from the green coast of Africa to the far white end of the world.

'You want to try'n sleep,' said the serang. He was worried about the boy. He had no faith in the stamina of young people.

Faraday shook his head. He was watching the sea.

'I'll be okay,' he said. His voice was a whisper in the wind. He rested his cheek on the gunwale and felt the spray on his face, collecting in his hair, running down his nose. The water beside the boat was dark blue, almost purple. There were long strands of pale weed on the sides of the boat, just below the water line, and small barnacles. A swarm of tiny silver fish, almost transparent, were feeding along the planks. They swayed in unison with the motion of the sea, moving like one body in the water. They moved slowly past him and then scattered suddenly, the shoal-body bursting apart, racing jerkily down into the blue water. He wondered what had frightened them, what strange secret smell, sight, or tremor of the alien sea. The sea seemed suddenly very deep and utterly terrifying and he felt his hands tighten on the gunwale.

He knelt there for a long while, looking down into the sea. A jellyfish lilted slowly by, swaying gently, a delicate tracery of pink and black, bobbing in the swells, the attendant little piebald fish peering shyly from between the poisonous folds of their host's lacy mantle. The jellyfish drifted slowly astern, bumping against the hull, rotating quiveringly, and vanished into the blue.

The Harvards passed far to the north. The boy heard them first, the familiar droning drifting down on the wet wind. He sat up screwing his eyes against the spray and wind and looked north. Far far away stray sunlight winked briefly from a canting wing and then the drone ebbed and faded across the waves and the sky was empty again. Faraday sat silently for a long minute, looking after the vanished aeroplanes. He felt sick.

'They'll come back,' said Pillay. He felt bad himself but he had great faith in the aeroplanes.

'They'll come back. Perhaps they just run out of petrol. They'll come back.'

The boy lay down without speaking and pulled the canvas over his face. The sound of the Harvards was a thing he should not have had to bear. He lay under the stiff canvas in the thick tar-smelling air. He wanted to be found most terribly now. All the excitement and the adventure were gone and now he just wanted it to end as quickly as possible. There were flashes of red light across the darkness when he closed his eyes and he wondered whether the sun and salt water had injured them. His head ached and there was a dull-sharp pain, like the stitch you get from running, just under his ribs. He sat up suddenly and stared wildly around. He thought he heard the Harvards again.

'Lie down,' said Pillay. 'Take it more easy, Boss. You just making it worse.'

'I heard the planes.'

'No. There's no planes yet. That's just the sea in your ears.'

He sat very still listening, turning his head back and forth across the wind but he knew all the time there were no planes. There was the rush and roar of the sea and the slapping of the spray and the creak of wood and the soft whine of wind around the wires but there was no big throbbing of an aero-engine.

Faraday lay down and slept. He slept like a nervous dog, twitching and whimpering.

The serang lay on his back and looked at the canvas roof over him and did not worry. He had given up worrying. He was quite resigned to die. All his life he had been resigned. He had done all he had to do, all he could do he had done. Now it was out of his hands. If he had to die now he would do it as well as he could, and he was a man who did well everything he tried. He was confident that if he had to die now, this day, out on this ocean in this boat, he would do so as well as possible. He did not particularly mind. This was not because he did not want to live, but because there was nothing he could do about it. It was out of his hands. It was like being in the navy again. There was nothing at all he could do about it and in a way he was glad because it saved him from a great deal of worry. He was worried about the boy however because he knew the boy would not be resigned to dying. He wondered if the boy was thinking about it. He wished he could make the boy resigned to dying because that would make it much easier for both of them. But the young are seldom resigned to dying and the young rich never. He thought of the boy's father whom he had only seen once and he felt sorry for him. He felt no animosity towards the rich. He had realised long ago that if you felt animosity towards the rich people or the white people – they were not always the same – your life was going to be one long frustration. So long ago he had grown a skin of indifference around himself and these things no longer bothered him. He felt resentment when whites half his age spoke to him as though he were a nothing, but this was because they were young and he was old, not because they were white and he was coloured. It was merely a matter of courtesy. He had no politics. He smiled at that, lying there in the dark under the stiff canvas.

'No politics and no ambition,' he said aloud. The hard stiff canvas brushed his lips when he spoke. He was of a generation of people who had had no politics and no ambition. There were not many of them left. He knew that way was changing now and he was glad he would not live to see the change.

'I would always be the same,' he said aloud, feeling the canvas against his lips.

'I would always be the same, if they would let me. No politics and no ambition, if they would let me.'

Well, he thought, you did have ambition, a small ambition, but still an ambition. You wanted a boat. That's an ambition. He remembered when he was working and saving for a boat. He lay there and remembered how he had walked along the quays at Kalk Bay, Hout Bay, Hermanus, and looked at the double-enders lying alongside, how he had loved the clean sweep of the clinker planking, the strong line of the stem, the scrubbed thwarts, the paintwork always fresh and glistening, the ropes coiled in the stern sheets. That was his big number one ambition. But ambition was like a flight of stairs: the landing at the top was the real ambition, but one went up a step at a time, achieving a whole lot of smaller ambitions along the way.

When he was pulling and hauling on the docks his ambition was to be a serang. When he was crewing in boats up and down the coast his ambition was to catch more fish than anybody else so that the pooled catch would be big and his share would be big and with the bonus for the biggest catch would give him enough to live on and maybe something to save. These were both small on-the-way ambitions which took him nearer his life's ambition.

When he first came to Bloubaai he worked in one of the big line boats. He worked every day. On days when his boat did not go to sea he filled empty places in other boats.

He lived in those days in a small shed behind the hotel. It was a small shed without lights or water and the hotel owner had let him use it for nothing. He still gave the hotel owner fish for that.

In those days he made extra money by catching the small octopus which lived in the rock pools and along the reefs. Night was the best time, with a low spring tide; night, or early morning when there was still mist on the sea. There was a good market for octopus, or *seekat* as they were called along that coast. The line-boats would buy them, or the sport fishermen would.

They were easy to catch: you tied a piece of rag to your gaff and trailed it back and forth before the over-hanging ledges in the rock pools. When the red rock crabs scampered out in terror, thinking the rag was an octopus, you impaled one of them and passed him up and down the rocks, past the deep cracks where the *seekat* lived. It wasn't long, usually, before a tentative tentacle would snake out. One quick thrust and hook with the gaff, a hard pull, before he could get himself truly entwined around the rocks, and whoops! It was a popular bait and a good one, and he made a few extra shillings out of that. That, and keeping the livers of all the small sharks and dogfish he caught and selling them to the trawling company. Most of the other fishermen were too lazy to bother about the small ones.

He lay and felt the boat move beneath him now and thought: he has really done very well, my *Poor Man's Friend*. Better than I thought he could, in such a sea. He patted the planks beneath him. If only the engine had not died. If only the engine was as good as the boat. But one could not have everything. He was by now very resigned and quite reconciled to losing the engine. The engine was very expensive and without it the boat was not much good but he had never felt anything for the engine.

The wind was fresher now and there were more whitecaps. The sea was jumping, the waves short and steep, confused. It became very wet in the boat. The boy woke up and sat with his legs pulled up. He looked very sick. There were scabs on his cheekbones where the sun had burnt on the raw flesh after the skin had peeled.

The movement of the boat was exhausting. The boat jumped and jerked and rolled and they could not lie down without bracing themselves with their arms and legs. Even when they sat they had to hold on to the thwart. The spray fell like rain and when it dried the salt made the skin itch. They both glittered with salt and their clothes and hair were stiff with it.

In the late afternoon they saw another ship. It was far away on the western horizon. They could only see it when the boat rose on a swell. It was almost hull down: just a smudge of smoke and sometimes the white of its upperworks.

It was in sight for an hour. They fired the remaining flares and hoisted the serang's shirt to the mast. The flares hissed dully into the sea and the shirt flapped once and then wrapped itself around the mast.

The ship went over the horizon and the wind tore away the streamer of smoke. The boy put his head on the thwart and cried aloud.

'Take it easy, Boss,' said Pillay. The boy sat up and wiped his face with the back of his hand. The tear marks showed on the sunburn.

'I'm all right,' he muttered. He was angry with himself for crying.

' 'Sno good us getting all upset,' said Pillay. 'They'll find us, sure thing.'

'When?' said Faraday. He looked around at the sea and the empty sky.

'They were so near,' he said. 'They were so damn near.' He meant the Harvards.

'They were so near. Why didn't they look this way?'

'Small boat like this's pretty hard to see in a sea,' said Pillay. 'Pretty hard. They've gotta have bloody good eyes to see us in these waves.'

'Pilots have good eyes. They test them. They've got to have good eyes. Those buggers just weren't looking,' said Faraday. He knew he was being unfair but he was so disappointed that he didn't care.

Thirst filled their mouths like sand. They could not keep their eyes away from the water tin. It was a green and white Castrol oil tin. It had held a good oil. Now it held a few pints of scummed water: tepid, tin-tasting, oily, but worth more than the most expensive all-purpose detergent friction-beating oil ever made. They sat and looked at the dented green and white tin, guilty with their thirst, and waited until it was time: time for a half-cupful, to be held in the mouth, swirled around, trickled slowly down the throat.

Clouds were piling in the north. The air there was very blue and clear along the horizon and the sea was black under the hard light. The clouds were piling in high white masses, pink at the edges. They looked very solid. You looked at them and you could feel the water gorging in them. They were flat along their bottoms, as though they had been cut off, and smoothly rounded on top. In the middle they were a bruised pearl grey. The clouds stretched like a wall across the northern sky. The sunlight streamed down from behind them like light through the slats of a blind. They were very beautiful but the serang saw no beauty in them. He knew they marked the current, where the warm air from the surface of the lukewarm Mozambique stream swirled upwards and con-densed. But seeing them to the north meant that the wind had pushed the boat through the current, southwards. He looked away south and imagined he could see the water change colour, feel it become colder through the planks of the boat. He sat and looked south and thought, down there is the very bottom of the world all blue and white and cold and it looks like we're going there, or will another current take us and spin us back again, or whirl us round and round this lower end of the world for ever? He unlashed the tin and unscrewed the cap. The boy slid along the thwart, watching the water greedily as it trickled into the mug. They took a long time over drinking.

And then, after the water, the milestone in their day, there was nothing to do but sit and count the hours to the next drink.

Later that day an albatross flew over them. It came up from the south-east, backing and veering wide and strong winged into the wind, riding the wind stiff winged over them, swinging back and forth over the boat, looking down at them with bead-bright eyes. They could see its feathers ruffling in the breeze and the small neat feet tucked up into the soft stomach feathers. It lost interest in them and whirled away on the wind, diving and soaring over the whitecapped sea. They could see it for a long way off and when it disappeared they felt lonelier than before. It was the only friendly life they had seen for a long time and they wanted it to stay.

13

Harry Koenig drove back from Port Elizabeth during the night. It was early morning when he arrived at the hotel they had moved to from the cottage. Thelma had refused to stay in the cottage. They had paid up the rent and paid the cook-boy a week's notice money and moved to the hotel.

It was the hotel they had drunk in the day the boat went missing. The bedrooms were worse than the lounge would have led one to expect. Harry got his suitcase out of the boot himself and went inside. The small foyer smelled like a bar which has had a lot of drinking and smoking done in it without any windows being opened.

He walked up the stairs to their bedroom on the first floor. The stairs creaked as he put his weight on them and the balustrade shook when he rested his hand on it.

Their room had a small balcony and French doors opening over the street. The room smelled like the foyer even though the window was open. It was already hot in the room. He pulled the curtains and left the passage door open. His wife was still asleep. She was one of those women who should always sleep alone with their bedroom door locked. She did not sleep well. Come to that, she did not awaken well, which is a thing some women can do, although not many, thought Harry.

Harry washed and brushed his teeth. He wanted a bath but in this hotel they never stoked the boiler fire before eight. He changed out of his creased clothes and put on khaki shorts and a khaki bushjacket and sandals without socks. Thelma woke while he was dressing and lay there with the sheet up under her chin like a bib, watching him.

'Nothing,' he said. He sat down on the bed. His legs felt weak. He was quite suddenly very tired and sick of it all. Thelma lay there without speaking.

'They had planes out,' he said. He felt he had to go on talking, to shatter the quiet between them.

'They were damn good,' he said. 'Everybody's been damn

good. They had the planes out from Port Elizabeth too, and today a big plane's coming up from Cape Town. Everybody's been damn good.'

'They haven't done anything,' said Thelma. 'They haven't done anything at all.'

'They did all they could,' he said. 'Believe me, they did all they could.'

'I suppose they gave you a drink,' she said. She sat up in bed and shook her hair loose. He looked at her and hated her and felt sorry for her at the same time for being that way and he knew it was the way she had always been and the way nothing would ever change, not time nor love nor money.

'No,' he said. He was determined not to have a row this morning.

'They did all they could, Thelma, and I'm afraid we have to face it.' God, he thought, how do I sound? Is that really me, enunciating so calmly, impersonally?

She started crying then, sitting there in the tumbled bed with the sun coming through the opened windows and showing up her face very badly. He sat there with his hands in his lap and wanted to put his arm around her, not as a gesture of love but a gesture of sharing, but he could not.

He sat there and felt something dwindling very small inside him at the realisation of what they had come to and he felt sick. There was a light sweat on his face and he felt sick. He felt this thing dwindling inside him and then he thought of the telephone call he should have made in Port Elizabeth but had not, and he was glad he had not. He looked at himself in the mirror over the dressing-table, tall, stooped a little, tanned, his face not showing the drink too much yet, his hair thinning, a tall quiet dark-faced man with fifty years crowding him just a little at this hour of a summer morning. He was glad that he had not made the call and together glad and sad and relieved at the sudden sure knowledge that he would not be making any calls like that ever again. I have now quit, he said, watching the face in the mirror. I have quit.

Thelma moaned softly. 'Farrie. Farrie, Farrie, Farrie.' He sat silently beside her, not touching her, watching himself in the mirror. Finally she stopped crying. She got out of bed, clutching her nightdress around her, standing wavering on the bare floor like an old woman.

He lay down on the other bed while she packed. His body ached with tiredness but he could not sleep. His mind bubbled behind the eyes' closed lids. He lay there and heard water running, splashing, drawers opening and shutting, the rustling of clothes. It seemed a long time before she said, in a small voice he barely knew, 'I'm ready, Harry. Harry!'

He sat up and squinted in the light. Their cases were standing in a row at the door. He stood up.

'Do you want to eat breakfast?' he asked, politely.

'I couldn't.'

` 'You should,' he said, conversationally. 'You should, you know.'

He crossed the floor and picked up the cases and she opened the door for him and they went down the dark, shiny-linoleum'd passage and down the stairs and into the foyer. The clerk was sitting dully behind the desk. Harry paid the bill and gave him the key and they walked out into the hot

131

street. He put the cases in the boot and slid behind the wheel. The seat leather was hot through his jacket. He pressed the starter and the big engine fired first time.

He sat there looking through the windscreen at the tumbled blue and white of the sea through the gap in the houses at the end of the street and thought about his son. Slowly he put the car into gear and they drove up through the town, just starting to awake now, and then they were out on the national road, climbing up through the orderly plantations of gums and pines and the sea was far below them. From here they could see the long swells coming in. He watched the grey road unreeling before them and saw the pines black on the mountain ridge and thought of trout streams in the Drakensberg and the green swells off Durban and the fresh gleam of rocks when the tide was falling in the early morning.

He drove up over the hills and away from the sea with his wife beside him and he felt lonelier than he had ever been and yet curiously uncaring.

'Are we going straight back?' asked his wife. It was the first time she had spoken since the hotel. 'Straight back to Johannesburg?'

'Yes,' he said. 'Straight back.'

And the funny thing was that this time he meant it.

14

They sat side by side in the boat. The fading sunlight was a warm yellow. The cloud bank over the current was very far behind them now. The high-piled masses were rounded and wind-sculptured, flushed pink in the sunset. The wind had dropped a little and the waves were only breaking sometimes, in a desultory sort of way.

Faraday picked up the green game-rod. He stroked the opaque green fibre gently with his fingers and wiped the damp film from the reel.

'Didn't do much, did it?' he said. He tightened the drag and spun the handles to see if it would run free. He was afraid that it had corroded.

'Good gear,' said Pillay. 'Catch many fish with it?'

'A few,' said Faraday. 'Some good ones.' He no longer wanted to boast to this man.

He looked at the rod and remembered the fish he had caught with it.

The big tunny off Cape Point: he had fought the bluefin for an hour, playing it very well, and then, right beside the boat, a mako shark had come up out of the deep blue, fast and straight, and bitten it in half. His father had shouted and thrown a beer bottle at it as it worried the tunny. Everyone on the boat had laughed and Faraday had joined in, but he was sorry to lose the tunny. The piece they boated had weighed forty pounds. His father had been more disappointed than Faraday.

Once he had caught a sailfish. That was off Durban. He was only fourteen then and his father was terribly proud. It was only a small sailfish, really, fifty pounds, but it had jumped a lot, fanning its wide sail, beautiful in the clean sunlight on the bay, and it had felt like a whale to him. Thinking of it now, it seemed that his father wanted him to catch fish more than he wanted to catch them himself. He always saw that Faraday had a good bait and a good position in the boat and he would always check Faraday's gear himself. He felt a quick rush of affection for his father, although at the time his father's attentions had made him impatient and a little embarrassed.

They had gone trout fishing, too, up in the Drakensberg where the water was ice-cold over the rocks, and the colour of brandy. It had come down from the peaks on the Basuto-land border. He didn't think trout fishing was particularly exciting but he liked the mornings in camp with the smell of bacon and coffee on the sharp high air and the soft chuckling of the stream over the stones.

He liked walking along the streams early in the morning, with dew glittering on the long grass and sparkling on the overnight spider-webs stretched across the paths. The morning mist lay a long while in the valleys, blanking down sounds. The plop of a surfacing trout sounded surprisingly loud. He liked walking along the quiet paths, putting his feet down carefully on the banks, and looking up and up towards Basutoland and seeing the high dark folded mountains always there, sometimes with thin clouds around them, sometimes with late snow very white against the rocks. One day, he always said, he would climb them, go over the top through the snow to Basutoland, to Mokhotlong and Teyatateyaneng and the other Basuto towns with strange, Oriental-sounding names.

They fished along rivers with strange names, the Moordenaars, the Berg, the Dooiemansdrif, sometimes with friends of his father's, more often alone. He preferred it when they were alone. Sometimes they took the little four-ten shotgun along and shot the quick red-legged pheasants which lived in the thick bush near the water. They only did this when there were no trout, or when they were tired of canned food. They were, above all, fishermen.

Now those days were dim cool memories. He remembered lying in the tent and listening to the night wind stir the leaves. He lay there listening to the wind tap the branches against the canvas and imagined it gusting down the dark valleys from the high peaks white with snow in the starlight.

Those were the days when there was very little bad feeling in the land and the few Africans they passed on the quiet dirt roads stepped aside and raised their hats and smiled their big white smiles and said 'Molo, Baas, Molo, Basie,' and 'Ow!' with admiration for the fish caught on a little bit of feather.

He sat there in *Poor Man's Friend* holding the game rod and thought of the bush and he badly wanted to go fishing with his father again.

It was the first time he had wanted to go fishing with his father for a long while, and he was sure the desire would remain with him even when he was ashore. He remembered his father's face when he had caught his first big fish and his father's pride when he had fought the sailfish well and brought it alongside the boat off Durban and how his father had gaffed it himself, taking the short-handled gaff from the skipper, not trusting anyone else with his son's best fish.

Those sea days were quite different in all ways to the mountain trips. In the bush and along the streams in the mountains everything was quiet and calm and muted. The sea days were yellow and white and blue and noisy and oil-smelling and sun-jumping green. They were quite different pleasures.

He remembered the return to harbour in the late afternoons when the wind had dropped and the sea heaved dully. He liked the healthy tiredness after a day on the sea, his face stiff with new sunburn. The boats skimmed smoothly across the shining harbour and the gulls fought and screamed over the offal drifting astern.

Yes, he wanted to go fishing again, but not for some time. Not for a long time, perhaps, but he wanted to go again. But in the beginning it would be the bush and the inland streams. He had had enough sun and salt sea for the immediate future. He lay back and thought about the present. That was a mistake, he realised. If you could not enjoy it you should endure it without thinking of it too much.

He wondered what the Malay, the big silent Malay, was thinking about. That was a departure. He was now old enough to realise that was a departure. They thought? He turned to him with sudden quick friendship. The Malay was sitting very erect, staring at the sea. He put his finger to his lips and pointed with his other hand.

15

Fifty yards away a dark shining back with a high spear-blade fin heaved through a wave-top and a deep wet sigh fluttered across the water. Faraday opened his mouth to speak but something in Pillay's eyes stopped him: that, and the dark menace of that tall dark fin, black against the sky like a far-off sail at sunset. He watched the shining sleek back porpoising through the swells and felt the sudden coldness of fear deep in his stomach when it turned and swam towards *Poor Man's Friend*. It was thirty feet long, blunt snouted, dark grey-black, with a gleam of whiteness showing below the water and it swam very purposefully, straight for the boat and the two watching men, driving down hard with the wide-fluked tail, puffing a misty breath when it surfaced. They could see the blowhole on the wide head opening and closing, winking like a lashless eye.

'Killer,' breathed Pillay, pulling Faraday down so that only their heads showed behind the gunwale. 'Killer.' They knelt on the boards and watched it come. Faraday felt his heart beating in his ears. The killer went down under the boat and his stomach flushed hot and then cold and the blood hissed in his ears and something tied itself into a tight ball under his ribs.

They sat very still until they heard the gusty phooo of the killer surfacing beyond the boat. Then they saw the other whale, a smaller one, twenty feet long, with a shorter fin.

When it lifted on a swell they saw it through the clear green water: heavy-snouted, high backed, dark shining slate with a white belly, driving hard and fast through the sea with quick excited down-thrusts of wide flukes. It slid down the smooth slope of a high swell and the fin sliced the water with a faint hiss and the killer's blowing was a soft phhhhhoooo across the water.

'That's his mate,' said Pillay. 'That's the cow-whale.' He lifted his head and looked around at the broken sea. He hoped there were no more. Two alone were not usual. They usually swam in small schools. He knew they could be very bad things to meet, far from shore in a very small boat.

Faraday watched the cow sweep past them. He was more fascinated than afraid now. He had never seen a whale before. He had seen their skeletons in museums, huge white bones dangling from the roofs. He sifted mentally through his big library of animal and fish books. *Arthur Mee's Children's Encyclopaedia, A Pageant of Animal Life, Wild Life of the World*, and dredged up a horrifying picture: three men sliding helplessly off an ice-floe which was being tilted by two high-finned black-and-white whales. Now he saw the picture clearly, and the caption: the grampus or killer whale, orca orca, a fierce, voracious mammal which attacks anything in the sea, including its fellow whales, and has been known to attack Arctic explorers by smashing ice-floes and throwing them into the water. They savage the young of other species, and rip out their tongues ... resolutely he closed the book and put it back on the shelf. That wouldn't do at all. You just couldn't think of things like that. But he was cold all over and his stomach was fluttering. All that stuff about a cold shiver down your back's so much bull, he thought. It's your guts that go first.

The big one came up steeply near the cow. They heard it blow hard.

'Go on, you bastards,' said Pillay. '*Voetsak*. Go 'way and leave us alone. We don't want you 'round here.'

He saw the growing fear in the boy's eyes and tried to smile reassuringly, but his face was stiff with tension and his mouth only twisted in a humourless grimace.

The whales were side by side now, bumping together in the swells. The water bubbled up between them in small jets and gushes, like the sea surging through a waterlogged hulk. Then they turned and swam towards the boat, a little apart, swimming very straight and fast and purposefully. Forty feet away they sounded, going down very steeply through the dark water. A trail of bright bubbles fluttered up after them.

Pillay imagined them diving down down down beneath the boat, turning on their wide tails far below, their small evil pig-eyes watching the little boat above, a tiny matchstick on the dancing silver ceiling of the sea . . . there was a sudden sweat on his face. *Liewe God, Liewe God*, please make them go away and keep going, please my *Liewe God*. It was the first time in his life that he had ever asked God for anything and now he was glad that he had not wasted any prayers in the past.

Faraday made a small sound of fear beside him. The boy was kneeling, clutching the gunwale with both hands, looking at the water where the whales had sounded. His mouth was open and his lips had cracked again and there was a bright red thread of blood fresh on his chin.

The whale hit the boat amidships with a solid chok! and *Poor Man's Friend* lurched and lifted in the water so that the sea came in over the port gunwale and there was a sharp snapping from the planks along the keel. The boat lurched heavily, as though it were being lifted, and then fell back wallowing into the sea and the whale had gone away. The boy's eyes were very wide and he looked at the sea with a kind of horror in his face as though it would vomit another monster.

'Jeez,' he said. 'Oh, Jeez. What – ' and then he saw Pillay's face and the fear naked on the man's face silenced him and he just knelt there silently, hanging on to the gunwale, watching the sea and waiting.

Pillay opened the locker and took out the lifejackets and he took one without argument, slipping his arms through the loops and lacing it across his chest, under the square cork floats, lacing it good and tight because he did not want it to ride up around his neck when he was in the water, and even while he was lacing it up he was thinking what good, what bloody stinking good is this because when we're in the water it will be all over and they'll come up wide-mouthed and toothy and snap our legs off as they dangle in the water. But he tied the belt tight and felt the coarse canvas rough against his skin. He felt better then.

The sun was low down now, pale behind the thin wind-cloud, and the foam on the small wave-tops was pink. Behind them, when he turned, he could see the very tops of the high clouds over the current.

The second whale came clear out of the water with a wild snorting grunt, nosing the boat's stern high and breaking planks along the keel. The bow went down as the stern came up and water came in over the gunwales and the boy fell forward with a high little cry of fright and then there was a last orgasmic heave and water foamed white around the stern and something broke with a high sharp metallic crack and there was a wide fluke black against the sky for a second, black and wide as a house against the pale sky, and then the boat fell back, rocking, broken, but floating.

The man and the boy were sprawled on the boards. They clutched the thwarts and pulled themselves up again, watching the sea, waiting for the other whale to hit them. The boat steadied and the rocking stopped and there was only the movement of the sea. The wind whistled in the wire rigging.

Two hundred yards away the sea boiled white as a big body crashed through a wave. They saw the sunlight on a broad back as the whale surfaced again, bursting through the swells.

'Look,' shouted Faraday. 'Look. Oh, Jeez, look at that!'

The bull came up again, tearing the sea, in a geyser of foam. He was porpoising very fast, almost hurling himself clear of the water. They could hear the loud thwack of his flukes as he dived. When he fell back it was like a shell burst on the sea.

'There's the cow,' said Pillay. She was swimming with less panic, but very hard and fast, swimming shallow and blowing hard. She was a hundred yards away and opening the distance between her and the boat rapidly. They watched both whales until they were out of sight. The splashing of the bull could be seen for a long way across the twilight sea. When the whales were gone they sat without speaking, letting the fear seep slowly out of them. They took off the clumsy life-jackets, smiling at each other, half-ashamed at wearing them, and Pillay's big hands trembled when he put them in the locker.

Faraday's face was fear-blotched through the tan. He sat there clenching his teeth and holding very hard on to the thwart. He was unable to believe that it was over. The size and power of the whales was something he could never have imagined. He shook his head and when he spoke there was a gasp in his voice. He was like a man in shock after a car smash. His hands felt as though they would flop around, beyond his control, if he didn't hang on to something.

'The bastards,' said Pillay. 'The bastards. The big bastards.'

'They nearly had us,' said Faraday. 'They nearly had us. Did you feel the boat lift? Man, it was nearly gone. Man, it was nearly over and gone.' He was laughing a little and very near hysteria. He sat there clutching tightly to the thwart and shaking his head and half-laughing and wanting to cry at the same time.

Pillay stood up. His legs felt soft at the knees, as though he had just got up after a long illness, and his head felt funny, light, as though the blood was draining out of it. His hands were still jerking. He went aft and saw that the tiller was hanging at a crazy angle and guessed the whale had hit the rudder and bent the pintles. He leaned over the side and saw the shattered rudder, a few pieces of torn wood, and then, below it, the bright gleam of fresh-snapped metal where one of the propeller blades had snapped off near the shaft. So that was it.

'Look here,' he said. 'Look where that devil hit himself.'

The boy lifted his head and looked at him without interest. While the whales were around his fear had made him forget his tiredness. Now he felt bad again.

'The prop,' said Pillay. 'That old killer, that old *mannetjie*, he snapped a blade right off.' He chuckled. He was feeling good. 'I'll bet he's got a hell of a headache right now. Oh, man, but I'll bet his head's sore right now.'

He felt very good about it. He felt *Poor Man's Friend* could still fight back, that they had not given up yet. He was not worried about the broken propeller. He could pick one up in the boatyard at Bloubaai for a few bob. It was worth a blade to get rid of the killer. At least, he modified it, it will be worth it if we get back. But he felt almost confident now, for the first time in days. He thought of the whale running into the sharp propeller blade with its head and he chuckled again. He was still chuckling a little hysterically when he saw the water rising silently over the floorboards. He stopped chuckling and sat very still, watching the dark oily water bubbling up through the boards as the boat rolled. It came in very fast and soon there was an inch over the boards and he could see it rising.

He knelt and lifted the floorboard and saw the gaps along the keel where the planks had sprung. The sea showed light green through the gaps. He put the boards back and stayed kneeling there in the water, thinking. The boy looked at him: 'What is it?'

'We're *klaar*,' said Pillay. 'That's what it is.' He stood up slowly, stiffly, and sat on the thwart. He felt all the strength, all the reserve of endurance which he had been nursing so jealously, ebb slowly away. He felt like a tired old man. He was too tired to go on. He just wanted to sit there and let the sea creep in.

Pillay got up again, slowly, painfully, and tried the pump. The handle was stiff and the plunger was blotched with rust.

He got a tin of grease from the locker and smeared it on the plunger with his fingers. He primed the pump with sea water and began to pump. It was hard work.

The boy was watching the water in the boat.

'We're leaking,' he said, almost conversationally. The pump made a high metallic grating. It was getting dark and the wind had dropped altogether but the waves were still breaking with sudden slopping noises. In the faint yellow and green twilight the crests were very white, almost luminous. There was a line of very clear sky low down in the west with a star in the deep indigo above it. Pillay leaned heavily on the thwart and pumped. The hot pain had come back to his chest and he felt really bad now. He was bitterly angry with the whale now. He thought it was a bad thing to be so angry with a dumb animal but he could not help it. Damn him, he thought. Damn and blast him bitterly and savagely to hell, the big bastard. Why must he do this to us? Why must he pick us for his games? He looked at the water in the boat and wondered if the boat would float if she was fully flooded. She had small buoyancy tanks fore and aft. He had put them in himself. But he didn't think they'd float the boat with the engine and two men. Not with the engine, he thought. The engine must go. He stopped pumping and Faraday took the handle. The water, rusty and oily, jetted out over the gunwale in unsteady gurgles.

Pillay opened the locker and groped around in the dark until he found the heavy shifting spanner. He lifted the floor-boards, opening them along the middle join and leaning them against the gunwale, and felt around the engine mounting until he found the heads of the bolts holding the engine block to the keel. It was awkward work in the dark and the wrench kept slipping. When the four nuts were free he uncoupled the propeller shaft and pushed it astern and bent over the engine, putting his arms around the block. It was very heavy and slippery but together they managed to manhandle it out of the engine compartment and on to the gunwale. They balanced it there for a few minutes, panting, the sweat drying on their faces, and then they tipped it over the side. It went under the dark water with hardly a splash, and they felt the boat rise in the water. Pillay leaned on the gunwale and looked at the water. The pain in his chest was still there but it was duller now, duller and deeper inside. When he lifted his head the stars swung dizzily around him and he sat down hard and rubbed his eyes.

They could feel the boat was riding better now. She was bouncing on the small chop which the rising night breeze was kicking up. Pillay sat and let the pain in his chest fade and thought of the whale with hatred. Of all the things to happen. Of all the things that could have happened this whale had to happen and kill his boat. Because he was sure now that this was the end. Anyway, it was the end for him. No matter what happened now it did not worry him. His boat was no good on that coast without an engine and he at his age could not buy another. It had taken him all his life to buy the engine he had just thrown over the side and he could not start again. He wondered why he had bothered to throw the engine over the side. I am no good without my boat, and my boat is no good without the engine, he thought. I do not care whether I die or not. I should have kept the engine in and died with *Poor Man's Friend.*

'She's floating better now,' said Faraday. There, thought Pillay, there is a reason. But it didn't make him feel any better. I should feel good about it now, he thought. But he didn't. He knew he was beaten now and defeat sat heavy in his stomach like stale sea-water, flat and sour. The empty engine housing gaped like a new scar in the starlight, the four long bolts sticking up from the hole like thick black sutures.

'You c'n stop pumping,' he said to Faraday. She may hold for a while now, he thought.

'I'm sorry about the engine,' said the boy.

'We had to,' said Pillay. He was thinking of his pride when the engine was first swung into his boat by the hoist at Bloubaai, brand spanking new, just out of the box, shining steel and green-painted cylinder head, his new engine, expensive, hard-working. It had never let him down before, never before that afternoon five days ago, and now it was rusting on the bottom. He wondered if it had reached the bottom already, or if it was still drifting down through the dark secret sea, turning over and over.

'Perhaps you can pick up another,' said Faraday.

'Perhaps.' With what, he thought. He wondered what the boy would consider cheap. What was money to him? Fifty pounds would be cheap to him. Fifty shillings would be expensive to a fisherman on the coast. He marvelled at the way money was distributed in the world. Some people had so much and most people had so little. It was never just right and he could not understand why God, who was said to have planned everything, could not have planned this better. He could not understand it but he had always been too shy and too aware of his own ignorance to ask the dominee about it. He looked at the boy's expensive game rod with the big Penn Senator reel and wondered how much that lot had cost. Probably more than the engine which had just gone over the side.

The water was gaining again. It crawled slowly up until it was level with the thwarts. *Poor Man's Friend* was too heavy to ride the waves now. She wallowed sluggishly through them and the small seas broke solidly against her and slopped over the gunwales. The wind was up again, whistling through the wires and buffeting the sea and the water around their knees was as cold as liquid ice. They were very far south of the current now and the cold they were feeling was the deep eternal cold of the Southern Ocean. There was the breath of the deep south on the wind and soon they were shivering so much that they could not speak. They had to clamp their jaws hard to stop their teeth chattering aloud. The sky was high black and cold and the stars were unwavering points.

16

During the night *Poor Man's Friend* settled deeper in the water, as though she was tired. She rolled heavily, like a sodden log, in the short seas. She took a long time to come back after each heavy roll, and Pillay knew she would go right over if a big wave hit her. He wished the whale had not smashed the rudder. But without engine or sail the rudder was not much good.

Now they just had to take it. In the dark they could not see the waves any more: just an occasional flicker of white in the dark, a rushing of wind in the dark, a tearing of water under the cold uncaring stars, and water swelling and tugging around them, water icy numbing cold so that they could no longer feel their legs. They sat across the boat from each other arms around the stays, and pulled their bodies small, withdrawing themselves into the body's last storehouse of warmth.

If I were alone, thought Pillay, I would die just about now. It would not be too difficult. I would just let myself go and die. He looked across at the boy. Perhaps he is thinking the same thing. Oh, we are a courteous couple. Please, may I die first? Oh no, after you, my *basie*. I'm going off my head, he thought.

Across the boat Faraday hunched in pain and cold against the hard wire. He looked at the bulking figure of the Malay, ragged against the stars, hooked crooked-arm around the stay like a tattered, storm-tossed bird. We're going to die tonight. It was as though somebody had whispered it in his ear, somebody sitting on the thwart between them. We can't, he whispered back. I will not. I refuse. We should sing or play games, he thought. He had seen a lot of war films. People always did that, or there was always a humorist aboard, does this happen every trip, any more for the Skylark?

'Talk,' he said to the night and the sea. 'We must talk.'

Pillay stirred, unwrapped his arm from the stay. Faraday saw his teeth flash in the starlight and thought, incongruously, I should love to have teeth like that when I am his age.

'We must do something,' said Faraday. 'We musn't just sit here.'

'Talk, then,' said Pillay. 'I'll listen. Promise I won't go away.'

148

He looked across the boat at the boy there hunched and cold, and thought, he really wants to live, this rich white boy. I don't care much any more but he wants to live. The starlight fell on the boy's thick hair, bleached yellow by sun and salt. It looked almost white in the starlight.

'Tell me about fishing,' said the boy. 'Your kind of fishing. Tell me about fishing out in the deeps, on the line boats.'

So Pillay told him about fishing far out in the deeps, off the East Coast and in the cold water off the west coast, where the mist lay low on the sea. Out in the deeps where your line took five full minutes to hit bottom, even with an eight-ounce lead, and where the stockfish came up all goggle-eyed and pulpy, with their swim-bladders forced out of their mouths obscenely by the change in pressure. And of other days when big sharks followed the boats and snatched every decent fish off the lines; and if it wasn't sharks it was seals, and the seals were worse because they were more intelligent and never came close enough to the boats to be harpooned or hit with bottles or sticks, but kept away, swimming in wide circles around the boats, watching the fishermen with their brown intelligent dog-eyes, waiting until a big fish was hooked, and then diving deep and taking it right under the boat. They never seemed to mind the hooks.

In early spring along the coast the fishing was bad. The sky was nearly always a dirty grey and quick sharp rain kept the boats damp and miserable and the only fish biting were the *doringtand* sharks, small sharks with a spine in the dorsal fin; for days there would be nothing but these small grey sharks, sometimes barbels or rays or on lucky days a stray *kabeljouw*; but most days it was just *doringtand* by the hundreds, so many, fin to fin on the sea bottom, that you could put on six hooks and catch six fish in six minutes, telling by the feel when each bait was taken.

Those days were cold grey monotonies of baiting and hauling and unhooking with the fish flapping and rustling and thwacking the deck and spilling yellow egg-fluid across the planks; and coming home, with the boat pitching and jerking in the westerly you gutted sharks, hundreds of sharks, with the seagulls wheeling and screaming over the boat, and the whole boat from stem to stern yellow and red-smeared and stinking of the sickly shark-smell which would soon turn sour, and the livers, yellow-red, blue-veined, quivered and glistened in the fish-boxes and the birds, gulls, and gannets and small sharp terns and chunky petrels fought and screamed over the offal spreading in the wake.

Then there was the calm night off Storms River when a big blue-pointer had come aboard. It was just before midnight and they were catching mackerel. They were going up the coast to the *geelbek* grounds at dawn and the mackerel were biting well. They were drifting a few miles offshore. There was a very low swell and no wind and they could hear the rising and falling roar of waves on the beach. It was very calm and they had slung hurricane lamps over the side from the boom and the mackerel were thick as driftwood on the water. They were catching them easily and quickly and keeping them alive in two big forty-four gallon drums of sea-water. The boat was a forty-footer out of Port Elizabeth, the *Dolphin*, a high strong boat with a flying bridge and wheelhouse aft and a long open deck. There were ten men aboard that night, leaning over the high ported gunwale and catching the swarming mackerel. They were all in good spirits, the night was quiet and warm. In the middle of the long deck a brazier was glowing red and over the fish smell you could smell coffee brewing. The only sound was the far-off surf and the gentle suck and whisper of the sea around the hull and the low murmurs of the men and the soft slapping and scrabbling of mackerel as they were swung inboard, shivering blue and silver in the yellow light.

It was all very peaceful and orderly and then the big blue-pointer came up out of the water. He was ten feet long and shovel-nosed, dark blue on the back and shining white along the belly and high-tailed and he came up out of the water and landed half across the gunwale with a splintering of wood and hung there for a second, writhing, wide-mouthed, snapping and twisting, and then he fell into the well-deck. The men scattered, screaming, below decks and into the rigging and some ran into the wheelhouse and shut the door. The big shark twisted and snapped and upset the mackerel drums and the deck was awash with sea-water and shark and shimmering mackerel. They waited until he grew weaker and then they came out of the wheelhouse and down from the rigging and attacked the shark with their fish-kieries, roping its tail to the mast. By this time they had got over the first shock and it was all rather fun and they made a party of it, laughing and joking. It was only when the shark was dead and overboard again and the mackerel back in the drums that they found one of the crew dead in a fish-compartment. The shark had fallen across him and bitten his leg through just above the knee, quite cleanly. He had fallen all folded up into the fish box and died there, with his severed leg lying across his

151

chest. He was always the quietest man on board and he had died the same way, lying in the fish box with his leg on top of him.

They took him out of the fish box and laid him on one of the forecastle bunks and then there was an argument about the severed leg, which was lying on deck, still wearing a grubby tennis-shoe. Some of the crew held that as he was already dead it did not matter what was done with the leg, and the sooner it was put over the side the better, but the others thought that the police would want to see the leg as proof of how he had died. (This argument raised the thought that they should have kept the shark as well). In the end they kept the leg, wrapped in dirty newspaper, and presented it and the body to a sleepy Railway Police sergeant when they docked early the next day. They realised that the whole thing was a mistake on the part of the shark. They had seen sharks jump before. This one had been coming up after the mackerel and his rush had carried him out of the water. It was just very bad luck that the *Dolphin* was in the way. They explained this to the policeman very clearly. The dead man's wife and children were on the jetty when they docked and they started wailing when the body and its attendant parcel were carried ashore on a stretcher.

The skipper went ashore and led them away and one of the white officials of the company which owned the line-boat drove them home in his own car. As the car-door closed the crew could hear the skipper saying that it really had been a mistake on the part of the shark.

When the family had gone the crew hosed down the deck and the fish-boxes and repaired the splintered gunwale. He had been a good fisherman and a pleasant fellow to have aboard but he was a man who always had bad luck and the feeling in the boat was that it was just the sort of thing which would happen to him.

While they talked the stars wheeled slowly overhead and the grey light crept across the sea. In the early morning the wind dropped and the sky had never looked so high or so cold or so deep and limitless with the stars hard points in the frozen air.

The sun came up slowly, pale through the low sea mist, and they came to life slowly. Faraday felt as though he had frozen to the stay. At first the wire had cut into him but now he felt nothing, nothing at all. His feet were dead and he wanted to rest them on the thwart but he didn't think he could lift his legs and he was afraid the boat would roll if he moved. It was full almost to the gunwales now. He wondered how long it would last if a sea came up and all his fear came back in a wave and he trembled with fear as well as cold. During the night he had wanted to pray but his mind had kept drifting off into sleep. He was still tired but now he had pushed it to the back of his mind and he felt quite light-headed. He tried to remember his prayers. His mother had always made him pray when he was small, every night, kneeling beside the bed with him, please God make me a good boy and please God bless Mummy and Daddy. It didn't seem like a very suitable prayer now. Then he remembered another child's prayer he had learned at Sunday school and he recited it under his breath, with his eyes on the stars.

There was no longer any sense of adventure or excitement or any hope. There was only the dull dirty taste of fear and sleeplessness and he was beginning to wonder how it would feel to drown. He imagined the boat slipping away from under them, nosing down with a bubble into the sea, and then the long drift in the lifejackets and the salt water slapping them in the face as the sea came up with the day until the water-logged jackets pulled them down.

Somehow, because he had never seen death, he could not imagine what it was like. He was glad about that. He looked at the Malay and wondered what he was thinking about. He felt sorry for the Malay. He thought it was a hell of a thing to lose your boat like this, when you were a poor man and had worked hard for it. If we get out of this, I'll ask Dad to see him right, he thought. Hell, my old man can buy a dozen boats like this. If he won't, I will. I've got money in the building society. He imagined himself drawing out all his money and buying Pillay a new boat and he closed his eyes and saw the scene so clearly that the tears squeezed out from under his lids at his sheer pure nobility. He opened his eyes and looked at the western sky, which was still dark with some stars just above the horizon. He wanted a drink. They had not drunk at all during the night because there was very little water left. He felt the thwarts and the gunwale to see if there had been a dew in the night but the wood was dry and cold.

'You want to try'n sleep now,' said Pillay. His voice was a hard dry croaking.

'You go aft 'n I'll go forrard and try'n balance her.'

'I'm okay,' said Faraday. 'Really, I'm okay. I'm just fine. I'm not tired.'

He shook his head as Pillay started to edge very cautiously forwards.

'Thanks, but I'd better not sleep. I'll just feel worse if I sleep.'

He could see the boat sinking under him while he slept, slipping slyly away from him and him struggling half-awake in the sea.

'I'll last,' he said. 'I'll last.' His voice sounded outside his head and he knew he was almost asleep sitting there.

He kept slipping off into vague dreams. To keep himself awake he told Pillay about his trip to Europe. He went there on a schoolboys' tour organised by a shrewd travel agent. It was designed for the sons of rich men. It had been his reward for passing into standard ten. They had flown to London and travelled over most of the Continent by train, to Brussels, Lucerne, Paris, Venice, Genoa, Rome, Florence, Vienna, Munich, Stockholm, the Tivoli Gardens in Denmark. They had seen the Seine, Notre-Dame, the Arc de Triomphe flood-lit with a huge tricolour fluttering below the arch, the girls along the Rue St Denis, snow on Rigi and across the lake the sun going down in the mist behind high snowy Pilatus, Madame Tussaud's, the yacht harbour at Monaco and they'd sat drinking Coca-Cola in the Piazza san' Marco while the orchestras thumped and the pigeons wheeled against the darkening sky.

'In Venice,' said Pillay, 'there are no cars?' He had seen travel posters of the city. It had always been a city he wanted to see. A man like him could live in a city which had no roads and no cars, only boats and water.

'No cars,' said Faraday. He told Pillay about Venice and he could see again the dirty crowded canal and feel the sun hot in the little squares with the bright canvas awnings and the tattered posters peeling on the ochre walls.

Back home they had boasted about the strip-clubs they had visited and some had hinted at even more erotic adventures. The nearest they had been to a strip-club was a daylight walk up Great Windmill Street with the young schoolmaster in charge of the party. He was a very serious young man who had wanted to be a priest and he was very embarrassed by the photographs outside the strip clubs and hurried them past at a trot.

He was not one of your modern schoolmasters. He thought the whole thing was absolutely disgusting and symptomatic of the decadence into which white civilisation was sliding. The boys did not share his views but they had a very tight schedule and they had no time to sneak back to Great Windmill Street. The next day they caught a train from Victoria station through Switzerland to Venice.

It was a dark four o'clock on a November afternoon when they left. He remembered the small party of boys huddled under the departures board on the cold platform, their breath clouding around them. The station was crowded, noisy, loudspeakers blaring, porters trundling loaded trollies through the travellers, the buffets full of people, windows steamed, puffs of stale liquor and warmed-up food gusting out through the swinging doors. He stood there, hands deep in his new and very expensive sheepskin-lined overcoat and read the names of the famous trains: the London – Paris, the Trans-European, the London – Basle, the Golden Arrow.

They took the boat-train to Dover, sitting dully in the non-smoker, watching the rain-misted fields slip by in the twilight. The channel ferry was crowded. By the time they got aboard all the inside seats were taken and they had to find a sheltered corner on deck. Some of the older boys tried to slip into the bar, but the schoolmaster was expecting that and herded them back to their deckchairs. A cold wind was gusting down the dirty grey channel and the ferry butted wetly through it to Ostende. The boys crowded the rail and watched the sad Ostende seafront, like a funfair on a wet Sunday, emerge from the rain-streaked night.

All that seemed years away now, years and years and years. He smiled when he remembered how they had complained about the hardships of that crossing.

Two years ago – it seemed two years since they had left Bloubaai, since they had put-putted out of the little harbour into the deceptive sea. Time seemed to be unwinding erratically, slowing down and speeding up ... he wondered what Pillay was doing while he, the schoolboy, was touring Europe ... in a town on the Cape coast where they had stopped for a week once there was an open-air fish-market in a dirty small street near the docks. The street was steep and very narrow, flanked by small grubby houses. At the top of the street, between two cheap hotels, was a smelly public lavatory and the fish-market. The fish were laid out on the kerb, among the drunks' spittle and the dogs' urine, for it was a street of dogs and drunks. The drunks dozed the day away in the sun against the wall of the lavatory. They were all old fishermen, too old to work in the boats, their bodies sagging, their eyes red damp sores in their devastated faces, their dying minds flickering dully through a fog of liquor. The whole street was very unwholesome and a great many letters were written to the newspapers about it but the drunks were the worst part of it, not because they were troublesome, but simply because they were there, sitting in the sun, every day, constant reminders of something.

On days when the wind was blowing from the sea the fish market could be smelt all the way into town. In the market square on windy mornings you could smell it.

Faraday looked at the old man and he thought of the drunks in the fish market and he shuddered. That was how they all ended. My father will do something, he promised himself. My father must do something. He wanted to say something to Pillay, something to express the friendship he felt, something to explain how their relationship had changed; but the words wouldn't come. His upbringing was like a wall between them. I'll make it right for them, he thought, squirming, inarticulate, I'll make it all right for him, oh-double-kay for him if we get out of here. His mind kept wandering off, skipping into other channels, but always he dragged it back, consciously, reining it in. He was still sure they would get back. Things like this just don't happen to me. People like me just don't get lost at sea. That happens to people you read about in newspapers, the whole faceless amorphous mass of others, the people to whom things happened. But I won't forget this I promise you, he said to himself, I'll stand up right there on the dock and shake his hand and it can appear in the newspapers and I'll do it and I won't care, even if my mother does pull her mouth and give me her oh Farrie look, because I bloody will do it. He felt very righteous and noble and his throat ached with his nobility. He closed his eyes and he could see the wind-blown quay with the reporters and the crowds and Table Mountain like a high grey and brown wall behind, and him shaking

Pillay's hand and walking with his arm around his shoulders to the car. This picture seemed to Faraday Koenig just then more daring and newsworthy than anything else, the sea or the blow or the whales or anything, because you can buck the elements, anyone can, but to publicly buck a whole seventeen years of teaching and living is something else again.

He awoke, trembling, as a wave hit the boat. *Poor Man's Friend* wallowed in the trough as the wave passed under her and the stern went down below the surface and the water came in smooth and green and glistening over the transom. They slid amidships to trim her and the stern came up slowly and then the water in her ran forward and the bow dipped. They moved carefully back and forth, sliding on their buttocks playing a dreadfully serious game of see-saws, until she was floating level, only shipping water when a swell disturbed her. They squatted on the gunwales, one on either side of the empty engine compartment and gazed blankly into each other's faces in the cold early light as the pale sun touched the tops of the waves. The sea was grey and shadowed behind the boat and the wind came up hard and sharp with the sun.

They sat dully, without speaking, and watched the sun rise. This is my last sun, thought Faraday. I know this is the last day. He could not feel his legs below the knees but it was not uncomfortable. The water which came up to his thighs was as cold as ice but his legs felt nothing. I should feel frightened, he thought. He let the thought stay in his mind and tried to assess it. I should feel frightened. But he felt nothing. Everything had the feeling of a dream now; you dreamed, you screamed in terror, you tried to run but your legs wouldn't move, and all the time a corner of your mind knew it was a dream, kept reassuring you that it was a dream, that you would wake up and the shapeless terrors would fade and the sun would be coming through the curtains and you could hear the street noises and the doves calling in the bluegums. And yet he knew this was no dream. He had been frightened many times before, in the last five days, but now that they were nearing the end of it he was no longer frightened. He had used all his fear and only resignation was left.

His resignation was born of the realisation that they were not going to die violently. When he had thought they were going to die violently, very quickly, roughly, and perhaps bloodily, he had been frightened, more frightened than he had ever been before. But now he knew it was not going to come that way, and it no longer seemed so terrible. It's all very well, he thought, to say a quick death is better than a slow one. That's what all the books say. That's what all the heroes want. The people who write that stuff have never been in a position to choose. When you are faced with it you always want to stretch it out as long as possible because if you hang on, if you're alive, there's always a chance, so you hang on with everything you've got to the very last minute and even at the very end you'll be looking at the sky and figuring there's still a chance and wondering if that's an aero-engine you hear. It will only be the wind in the rigging, but you won't know that disappointment. Besides, we never really believe that we, me personally, I, will die. It's always someone else. Right now, he said, I don't believe I'm going to die. Other people die. You read about it in the newspapers. Death, like sweepstake-wins, happens to other people.

17

Pillay sat and watched the oily water swirling around his legs. He thought the oil-colours were very pretty. He wanted to stir them with his fingers, to change the pattern, but he was too tired. He sat with his head hunched a little, watching the coloured water. He had stopped looking at the horizon a long time ago. He had no hope of being saved, or any real desire to be. He just sat and kept his eyes down in the boat and waited for the long slide down to begin. He had taken off his life-jacket and laid it on the thwart beside him. He wanted to go down with the boat. He sat and looked at the much-loved planks beneath his feet, the scar of the engine housing, with rust in red patches already on the long bare bolts, the scrubbed thwarts, smoothed by countless buttocks, the black-capped gunwales with the deep line-scores. Ah, I loved this boat, he thought. *Poor Man's Friend*, you bastard, you good strong faithful bastard, I hope you go down straight and deep, and I with you.

He raised his eyes, and saw the boy looking at him. 'She won't last long now,' he said. It was the first time he had admitted defeat and he was surprised at himself. The words just came out.

The boy looked away. He was angry with Pillay for mentioning it. He was superstitious and he thought you shouldn't say things like that.

'Anytime now,' said Pillay. He wondered why he was talking. He saw that it was upsetting the boy.

Faraday kept his head turned away. He thought it was wrong to talk about it.

'I'm sorry,' said Pillay. 'I'm sorry, Boss.' Suddenly he started laughing, softly at first, and then louder. His lips cracked and blood threaded down his chin, very red against the white stubble.

When he stopped Faraday was still looking away. They sat silently then, with the sinking boat between them, while the rising wind boomed across the sea.

18

Five hundred miles to the south the South African Navy frigate *Louw Wepenaar* was beating her way out of the tail-end of the Roaring Forties. She had taken a beating during the last three weeks, and the bruises still showed: a crumpled ventilator, a stoved-in whaler, crazily-twisted stern-rails, vivid splashes of red oxide paint on the grey. A routine trip down to the Marion Island weather station had turned into a slogging monotony of cold and monstrous seas and knife-edged gales, with tragedy at the end of the road: they had lost a petty officer and two ratings when a breaker had slammed the launch against Marion's cliffs. Now the frigate was beating sullenly back, bruised and bereaved.

The captain sat in his cabin this bright wave-tossed morning and drank his tea. He was very tired and the sunlight lancing through the scuttles hurt his eyes. It had been a long trip and it had drained a lot of life from him. He felt the need to be recharged, like a battery which has run down. He would be very glad when they came alongside at Simonstown. He closed his eyes and saw, as he had so many times this trip, the pleasant harbour, calm in the late afternoon, the warm white houses climbing up the red hillside, the two old destroyers swinging peacefully at their buoys. It would be good to come home. He poured another cup of tea and thought of the letters he would have to write to a mother and two widows. He did not have to. The Department would already have told them, in very polite officialese, that a misjudged wave had snatched all their hopes from them and smashed them against an unfriendly cliff in an ice-cold sea. He did not have to have anything more to do with it. But he would. He was that sort of man. He thought about the men. Three good men. What a waste. What a terrible mindless waste. He leaned back and closed his eyes. The bright chintz curtains fluttered in the breeze. It was a pretty cabin.

His wife had had something to say about the decorating of it. It was very chintzy and a little feminine but it was homely and fresh and the captain, who was a man of very little sophistication in non-naval things, liked it that way.

There was a tap at the door. The captain sat up, opening his eyes.

'Come in,' he said. A young seaman in blue denim working rig came in.

'Signal, sir,' he said. He was only a boy. The captain stood up and took the slip of paper from his hand, unfolding it.

'Thank you,' he said. The boy clicked his heels and went out, shutting the door carefully behind him. The captain read the message and then stood there, with the yellow paper in his hand. The ship rolled a little in the beam swell and the shafts of sunlight swayed across the cabin.

'Damn,' he said softly. He put on his cap and went out. Up on the bridge the wind was cold and the sunlight was very bright but without warmth. He stood looking out over the ice-blue sea, seeing the giant swells building up and rolling down on the ship, huge, inexorable, feeling the steady thrub-thrub-thrub of the engines pulsing like a heartbeat in the metal plates beneath his feet.

The first lieutenant and the navigating officer were standing out of the wind in the port wing. They were both very young men and the morning air had flushed their faces so they reminded the captain of schoolboys after a game of rugby. They saluted him, a little self-consciously.

'Got some work for you, Pilot,' he said to the navigating officer. He always called the young man pilot. It was a reminder of his war service with the Royal Navy. It was a title which was going out of use in the South African Navy and the captain tried to keep it alive. He was privately convinced that the people in Pretoria – to him the whole Government machine was personified by hundreds of faceless 'people in Pretoria' – were out to emasculate the navy, to whittle away its traditions and little foibles one by one, to reduce it to a sort of sea-going army.

'Sir?' The navigating officer was a young lieutenant with the big hands and open, slightly puzzled face of a farm boy who still doesn't quite know just how he got this rank, this ship, this uniform. He was engaged to a very pretty girl in Cape Town and the captain knew he was counting the days. Well, thought the captain, your little game's going to be delayed.

'It'll be a good exercise for you,' the captain said, with a malicious chuckle.

'Yes, sir,' said the farm-boy, without enthusiasm.

'You've got their last position, near enough. Check back on the weather reports for the last six days, see if you can work out where they've drifted to. Then give me a change of course, please. Soon as possible, Pilot.'

'Yes, sir,' said the farm-boy. 'Do you think we'll be delayed long, sir?'

The captain laughed shortly. 'Until we find them,' he said. The boy's face was quite blank.

'I see, sir,' he said. The captain crossed the bridge and picked up the microphone.

'I'm sorry about this, Number One,' he said.

'The men are pretty chokka, sir,' said the First Lieutenant. There was a flash of anger in the captain's voice.

'Can't be helped,' he said briskly. He stood there with the microphone in his hand, thinking of the ninety tired men whose pleasant daydreams he was going to dispel. He switched on the microphone.

'This is the captain speaking,' he said.

When he had finished he stood there looking at the sea. He could feel the resentment in the ship beneath him.

He shrugged and went down the steel ladder and along two narrow corridors to the bright chintzy cabin. I'm sorry, fellows, he thought, I'm truly sorry. I want to get ashore just

165

as badly as any of you do. The chintz curtains fluttered in the breeze and a few drops of spray pattered into the cabin as the frigate rolled. He got up and closed the scuttle.

19

They steamed north-east at full speed all that day and through the night and in the early dawn of the next day they turned west and a little south, rolling heavily before the long swells, radar sweeping the dark crinkled line of the horizon. When the sky was a clear water-colour pink in the east there was a sudden flare on the blackness of the radar screen.

The lookouts were doubled and the frigate steamed down on the bearing, her engines at slow ahead, just moving her enough to keep steerage-way. She was rolling very badly with the swells right behind her, slapping her square stern and making her yaw. Her mast raced blackly across the hard clear sky and the breeze hummed softly in the wires. The helmsman swore frequently as she wandered, feeling the ship through his fingers resting lightly, lovingly, on the big wheel with its brass-capped spokes. The figures on the gyro-compass repeater clicked backwards and forwards, on course, off again, on, off ... a little wheel, just a trifle – ah, she was coming back ... not too much, don't get her swinging the other way ...

Poor Man's Friend was very low in the water, so low that they almost ran her down, so low that the captain, looking at her through his glasses, was surprised that the radar had picked her up.

The captain watched them for a long time. The small black figures sat unmoving on the grey morning sea. He wondered if they were still alive. He bent down and spoke into the voice-pipe.

'Port ten.'

He wanted to overshoot the drifting boat and come up into the swell. The frigate swung across the waves, rolling more heavily. A giant swell rushed up her sides and foamed briefly along the deck. When they were down-wind of *Poor Man's Friend* they came about, lurching in the deep troughs, and steadied into the big swells. It was more comfortable now that the frigate was putting her bows into the sea.

The surgeon-lieutenant came on deck and the captain handed him the glasses. The surgeon looked and said:

'They're waving, sir.'

'Must've just seen us,' said the captain.

'Poor devils,' said the surgeon. They stood side by side without speaking and watched the boat grow bigger as the frigate approached. They were steaming very slowly. The surgeon handed the captain his glasses.

'We're ready for them, sir,' he said. He went back down the iron ladder and along the deck. The duty seaboat's crew were standing by and two seamen in lifejackets were in the swung-out whaler.

'How do they look, sir?' asked one.

'They're alive,' said the surgeon. 'They're waving.'

'That's wonderful,' said the seaman who had asked the question.

'It's a bloody miracle,' said his mate.

The surgeon went below. He was an army doctor who had been seconded to the navy for this trip. He had expected it to be a holiday cruise. He went along the swaying, hot-air and oil-smelling corridors to the small neat sick-bay.

His SBA was a professional seaman, and looked it. He was about forty, short and wide, with a bald head and a very carefully trimmed red beard. He took his job very seriously indeed and regarded himself as a man who would have been a doctor if there was any justice in the world.

'Tea, sir?' he asked.

'Thanks.' The surgeon sat and drank his tea and thought that he had drunk a lot of tea this trip. The navy was dry at that time and he hated soft drinks so he had turned to tea and now he drank about a dozen cups a day. He sat sipping his tea and thought that he would probably never go back to liquor. Then he felt the deckplates tremble in an altered key as the frigate went astern. He sighed and stood up.

'We may have some customers,' he said. He went out and as he climbed the ladder he heard the whaler being lowered.

20

When they saw the frigate they just didn't believe it. She came up silently out of the haze, half shrouded by her own smoke which was rolling down over her, the colour of the dawn sea except for the black funnel and mast. They sat looking at her. The frigate was beam on at first and then she turned. They could not see which way she was turning and they thought she was turning away from them and they stood up and screamed until they saw the curling white bow wave as the frigate surged on a swell and then it was all right and suddenly they both began laughing and slapping each other on the back. Then they grew silent and watched the approaching ship get larger and larger until she seemed to tower over them. They could see the men on the bridge and others crowding the rails and the whaler being swung out.

'*Dankie God*,' said Pillay softly, watching the frigate swing around them.

'*Dankie God*.'

They sat Pillay at the long, well-scrubbed table in the seamen's mess and gave him food and coffee. The coffee was steaming hot and sweet. He sat with his elbows on the table and held the cup with both hands. His hands were trembling. The seamen sat and watched him eat and drink.

When he had eaten a petty officer sat down beside him and gave him a cigarette. When he saw Pillay's hands he lit it himself.

'Was it very bad?' he asked. He was very sympathetic. The other seamen drifted nearer.

'We were finished,' said Pillay. 'And the boat was finished, too. She was really finished.'

'She took a beating,' said the petty officer.

'She's a good boat,' said Pillay, defensively, 'but the sea finished her.'

The frigate's engines were going ahead again and in the mess the shafts of sunlight swayed across the bulkheads as the ship turned.

'That's a hell of a coast,' said the petty officer.

'We're a long way off it now,' said Pillay.

'Yes. But that coast is a hell of a coast.'

'Worst in the world,' said a young seaman. 'I read in the papers where some guy said it's the worst coast in the world.'

'You want to shower now?' asked the petty officer. 'Shower and then a kip, eh? I guess you could do with that.'

He went away and came back with a clean white towel, neatly folded, and a square of yellow soap. Pillay stood up. His head swam a little and he shook it. The seamen looked at him with concern in their faces.

'I'm all right,' he said. 'I'm – '

Boompa-boompa-boompa went the Bofors. The sound came flatly through the open scuttles.

It was suddenly very quiet in the mess. In the silence the Bofors fired again, finally: boompa.

Pillay picked up the towel and soap.

'I'll take you to the bathroom,' said the petty officer. He led Pillay down a ladder and along a narrow corridor to the bathroom. Pillay pulled his jersey over his head and un-buttoned his shirt. The petty officer was still standing there watching him.

'I'm sorry about the boat,' he said.

Pillay shrugged. He was thinking of *Poor Man's Friend* the day he had bought her: the strong clean lines, too business-like to be beautiful, the light blue hull with the black-capped gunwales and the stubby mast shining with new varnish, the

170

rigging new and clean, the ropes all eyed or end-spliced, coiled neatly fore and aft . . .

'We couldn't leave her,' said the petty officer.

'We just couldn't just leave her drifting.'

'She was finished anyway,' said Pillay. 'She was gone.' He didn't want this young man to feel bad about it.

'We're all sorry,' said the petty officer. The sunlight shafted through the scuttle and lit up his square earnest face with its big freckles. His fair hair shone in the sunlight like the turnings from a brass lathe.

'You have a shower and a good kip and you'll feel better,' said the petty officer. He turned on the water and tested it with his hand.

'It's okay, he said. 'Sometimes it runs too bloody hot.'

He went out and Pillay got under the shower. He soaped himself and let the water rush over his head. He stood there under the rushing water looking out of the far scuttle at the sunlight on the racing sea and thinking of his boat.

The frigate rolled and he swayed against the bulkhead and leaned against it for a long while, with the hot water sluicing down his body, slicking his hair to his skull, running off his nose and ears and fingers in little jets and fountains. He felt tired and terribly low, lower than he had ever felt before. There was a mirror against the far bulkhead. He leaned against the cool water-dewed steel and looked at the grey-haired old man slumping in the far mirror. You're finished, old man, he said. Finished, *klaar*. You're no use for nothing any more. It was an effort to dry himself and dress.

Later when he was lying in the bunk (in a white man's bunk. In a white seaman's bunk, he thought. Me. Lying in among white men in a white man's bunk. *Liewe God)* he could not sleep. He lay there in the dimness under the warm sheets with the slow breathing of the men all around him and sleep would not come. Outside the sea hissed and whispered against the plates. When the frigate rolled he caught glimpses of fleeting white wave-tops, shining in the starlight. There was a wind on the sea and the waves were tearing their tops. Through the scuttle the sky was very black and the stars were hardwhite points.

He lay there and thought about the boy and wondered what the boy was thinking about. But the boy was probably asleep. He wondered if the boy had been up on the bridge when they shelled *Poor Man's Friend*, and whether the boy had cared. He wondered if the boy had cared at all. He lay there and the thoughts came crowding in so fast that they blurred into each other, a series of shifting images, like the first dream on the edge of sleep.

They had separated Pillay and the boy as soon as they were back on board. The boy had been taken down to the captain's quarters and he had been taken down to the seamen's mess. He didn't mind that. He was quite used to that. Anything else would have surprised him.

He slid quietly out of the bunk. The deck was cold under his feet. The whole ship was very quiet. He pulled on the clean overalls they had given him and padded out of the mess. In the companionway a light was burning but there was no-body around. He went up the ladder and out on to the deck. The wind was cold and the frigate was steaming right into it. He stood on the gently throbbing deck and listened to the rushing of the sea and the whining of the wind in the rigging

172

and the soft pulsing of the engine-room blowers. The night wind ruffled his hair and tugged at his overalls. He faced the bow and watched the mast swaying against the star-dusted sky. He walked slowly aft. The wake spread out astern like a gleaming, rolling fan on the dark sea. He leaned over the stern rail and watched the white water roar and bubble around the screws. Foam hissed along the steel plates and whirled astern into the tumbled luminosity of the wake. Outside the cone of the frigate's lights on the sea was a dark unfriendly plain. He looked out, straining his eyes into the dark, wondering how far away the land was. But the stars came right down into the dark sea and the land was below the horizon.

Well, he thought. Here we are, at the end of it all. Those wasted years. They might never have been. What is there left? A rented cottage. A few pounds in the post office savings bank. Some cheap furniture. Faded curtains. A dog that you can't afford to keep. All your life has suddenly unwound with a rush and you are left holding the end of the string and wondering where it all went and even your memories of the good days don't help because they just make the present harder to bear. He leaned on the rail and rested his head on his arms and felt an overpowering desire to cry like a very young child, wildly.

A man needs luck, and that's what I never had. I never had none at all. I did what my parents taught me, what the church taught me, I worked hard and I stayed decent and I never run my neighbour down, but I never had any luck and without luck a man's got no chance at all, just no chance at all.

21

The boy slept. He was on the couch in the captain's cabin. It had been made up into a bed for him. The wind fluttered the bright curtains and stirred his hair. He had bathed and eaten well and now he was sleeping well, without stirring, without dreaming.

He had never needed any luck.

22

They came in on a windy afternoon with the south-easter chasing up the whitecaps in the bay and unrolling the cloud over Table Mountain. The wind had blown away the smoke haze over the town and the air was very clear, except along the foreshore where the red dust was swirling from some building sites. The streets had that bare swept look which a bad wind gives to a seafront town.

The frigate tied up astern of a United States Navy missile recovery ship, an ugly conglomeration of olive-drab steel and hoists and derricks with two bright orange helicopters snared on her after deck like giant dragonflies.

There was a small crowd waiting impatiently in the wind on the quayside: as they came alongside Faraday saw his father and mother and two aunts from Cape Town. They stood there like people waiting for a circus to open, hands clutching hats, faces screwed up against the glare from the sky.

Pillay stood in the lee of a gun-turret. Crowds had always made him feel unhappy. He sheltered against the steel plating and tried to become as inconspicuous as possible, which was not very easy. He saw someone on the quay point to him. The crowd-eyes flicked to him for an instant, and then rotated upwards: he guessed they had seen Faraday on the bridge. He felt only relief at being no longer the focus of interest. He felt no resentment. They were no longer at sea now; he was back in Faraday's world. He was used to it. Anything else, any change in the order of things, would have alarmed him.

The gangplank was dropped and he followed the boy slowly ashore into the surging, welcoming crowd. Flash-guns blinked, reporters jostled, questions and orders showered on them: stand here, look this way, smile, look relieved, hold it, push pull jostle flash and a railway policeman, harassed and sweating in his khaki uniform, trying to keep the crowd off the railway lines and somewhere a baby crying in a long sustained reedy wail and on the edge of the crowd a very drunk fisherman gazing without understanding at the excitement and mouthing wine-blurred questions which nobody answered.

A tall tanned man with thinning hair was holding Faraday by the shoulders. The man's face was twitching with emotion. A plump woman of the type Pillay automatically classified as 'a rich *missus*' was trying to kiss Faraday and put both arms around him and use her handkerchief at the same time. Nearby

175

two other middle-aged women sniffled restlessly, weeping neither quietly nor gracefully. Faraday stood very tall and he seemed a long way from the desperately clutching family.

'Please move along,' said the policeman. His collar was a dark band of sodden cloth. Pillay looked at him and thought absently, they should let them wear shorts and open neck shirts in this weather . . .

The photographers came back.

'Over here, please, Mr Koenig, look this way please, Mr Koenig . . . let's have one with your arms around each other . . . that's fine, that's just fine . . . thank you . . . '

Flash.

Pillay looked at Faraday, wanting to catch his eye, wanting to say good-bye, even with a glance, but more people were welcoming him now and a dirty-legged little boy was being lifted up to kiss him . . . allemagtig, thought Pillay, but he has a big family.

The crowd enfolded Faraday joyously, wetly, weepingly, laughingly, a swirling breaker of faces, tear-stained, smiling, bobbing him along from hand to hand, kiss to kiss, hug to hug, a mêlée of emotion which was confusedly distasteful and gratifying.

Over the head of a sniffling aunt he saw Pillay wavering on the fringe of the crowd, the dark face seeming darker now on shore, terribly dark, the crisp hair crisper, whiter, crinklier, like Uncle Remus', the deep sad creases beside the wide mouth cruel scores in the hard light. Their eyes met and the serang smiled, carefully.

'Please,' said Faraday. 'Please,' pushing against the pressing bodies, insistently, yet with his hands falling away even as he

176

lifted them to clear a path.

'Please,' he said again. The white head was moving away now, withdrawing quietly, respectfully.

'Please,' said Faraday. 'Please. I must – ' They looked at him wonderingly, the good kind civilised white races, all smiles and drying tears, charity laid on carefully, dutifully, over three hundred years, layer by layer.

'I must get through,' said Faraday. 'Please. Please let me through.'

They fell away, reluctantly, hands still resting on him, kind eyes watching curiously, and as they parted he felt a deep flush coming up him, a deep adolescent flush coming right over him, hot in the pit of his stomach and burning on his face, and his feet dragging lead-heavy, molasses-mired as in a bad dream, his hands like dead meat by his side, brushing numbly against his denims: he stood, and he was glad when they clutched him again, drawing themselves hungrily around him.

The gap in the crowd closed and another opened and he and Pillay were swinging away from each other, faster and faster and faster, like the poles of a magnet, repelled by the same force which could have drawn them together. He saw suddenly and very clearly that what was impelling them so frighteningly rapidly away from each other was not the force itself but the realisation that there was a force which could repel man from man. But it throbbed between them now, the realisation of it, tangible, intransigent, and he knew that was the way it was and the way it would always be because it had been made that way.

He stood there remote from the crowd, tall and seventeen,

painfully aware of himself and hating himself deeply and hurtingly with the nauseous hatred of cowards, and when the crowd pushed him towards the car he went along with them, unprotesting, looking straight ahead and never turning back because he knew the time for turning back had come and gone and he had missed it for ever.

The crowd trickled away along the quay, towards the car-park near the goods sheds, and Pillay was left alone on the wharf. The cranes drew long shadows on the concrete. Far, far away a white speck dangled on the very lip of Table Mountain: the cable-car, waiting for the wind to drop.

He felt a sudden flush of panic, a terrible feeling of empti-ness, of flatness, of disorientation. The docks seemed vast and unfriendly.

The wet salty sea wind blew in from the bay and sent hats rolling and skipping down the quay and old newspapers fluttering like leaves around the moored ships, down finally to join the garbage in the scummy harbour, the city's pride, awash with orange peels and beer bottles and broken fruit-boxes and water-logged fish baskets and ice-cream cups and less mentionable things bobbing and surging back and forth on the careless tides.

There was nothing for him here. He began to walk along the quay towards the dock gates. They had been loading maize and the concrete was gravelled with the big white kernels. He was amazed at the casual way things were wasted in the harbours. In any harbours. In Port Elizabeth he had seen the waters dotted with oranges. In East London it had been pineapples. These things came back to him as he walked down the quay.

He had a vague idea of walking up to the national road and getting a lift towards the Garden Route, to Bloubaai. There was very little left for him there, but it had been his home for a long time and he wanted to see it again.

He looked up at the blue and green and brown hills behind the tall modern buildings and stepped out more determinedly. Perhaps it would not be so bad. Far up on Signal Hill he saw the grey-brown smudge of a bush fire.

Somebody was calling him. Well, not him, exactly, but they were calling 'hey', loudly, and with a tone of voice which suggested that it would become 'boy' next. He stopped, turned. The tall tanned man, Faraday's father, was striding long-legged towards him.

Pillay waited, awkwardly, his big hands dangling at his sides. He did not know what this man wanted. He did not especially want to know.

'Hey,' said the man, more friendly now that Pillay had stopped. He stopped, hesitated, started again, stopped once more, looked around.

'You're the fellow – you're the man – ' he said.

'Yes,' said Pillay.

They stood there looking at each other on the windy quayside, squinting in the glare, the gaunt cranes clanging and whirring above them.

'Sorry we neglected you,' said the man. He gave a short laugh, but stopped hurriedly. He lifted his arm as though to shake hands, thought better of it, and adjusted his sun-glasses.

'The wife was pretty upset, you know,' and the man stopped again. Why don't you say Madam, thought Pillay.

'Didn't mean to forget you,' said Koenig, and gave that

short unhappy laugh again. He looked over his shoulder quickly, as though to reassure himself that he was not being watched.

'That wouldn't do, would it?' asked Koenig, brightly. He was really trying very hard. He wanted to leave now. He wanted it all over and done with.

Pillay stood silent. In the bright light he looked very old.

'My wife and I – that is, my wife and I, we want you to know that we're very grateful, very grateful, for the way you looked after our boy,' he said.

'We won't worry about anything else, will we?' And don't let's have any nonsense about compensation or any damn fool ideas like that, his eyes said. He pressed a piece of paper into Pillay's hand and turned away abruptly, walking rapidly over the quay with long, almost hasty, strides. The set of his back told more than his face ever could have.

Pillay opened his hand and looked at the green rectangle of printed paper.

It was a cheque for twenty pounds.

Suddenly he began to laugh. He tore it across, again and again, slowly and without anger, and dropped the pieces into the harbour. They fluttered gently down, a small grey gull swooping hungrily after them.

'Hey,' said a new voice behind him. He turned with a nervous start. It was one of the photographers, a young, pleasant-faced man with short fair hair and a pink skin.

'Say,' he said again, 'What'd he give you? What'd Mr Koenig give you?'

He leaned over the edge and saw the scraps of paper floating on the water.

'Say,' he said, excitement making him stutter a little, 'Say, th-that looks like a – '

Pillay turned and walked up the quay, faster and faster, until he was almost running. The photographer watched him go. Then he shook his head and walked back slowly to his car.

The crowd had all gone now and the gulls and tall cranes which looked like huge metal storks were the only things moving on the windy quayside.